Tommaso Salvini

Leaves from the Autobiography of Tommaso Salvini

Tommaso Salvini

Leaves from the Autobiography of Tommaso Salvini

ISBN/EAN: 9783337029159

Printed in Europe, USA, Canada, Australia, Japan

Cover: Foto ©Raphael Reischuk / pixelio.de

More available books at **www.hansebooks.com**

THE AUTOBIOGRAPHY
OF TOMMASO SALVINI

TOMMASO SALVINI AT THE AGE OF TWENTY-NINE.

THE DE VINNE PRESS.

ILLUSTRATIONS

LEAVES FROM
THE AUTOBIOGRAPHY OF
TOMMASO SALVINI

RECOLLECTIONS OF MY YOUTH

WHEN I was a little boy I ran away from home because of some fancied harshness, and three days later was found in a distant city and brought back by our old family servant. My father's bearing toward me after this escapade made a profound impression on me; for, instead of punishing me severely, he chose to pass my misdeed by in absolute silence. His kindness caused a complete change in my boyish character, and I resolved to be a source of trouble to him no more, but to seek in every way to gain his esteem and love. I remained with him a year after this, and I have the satisfaction of feeling that during that year I was scrupulously obedient and attentive to my duties.

My father saw that it would be impossible for my brother and me to make serious progress in our studies in the midst of the nomadic life that we were leading with his theatrical company, and he determined to place us at Florence with our uncle and aunt, and to send me to the Law School, and my brother to the School of Fine Arts. It was my father's wish that I should be a lawyer, and my brother a painter. Our uncle and aunt lived in the Via Romana, near the gate of the Boboli Gardens, and it was not pleasant, especially in winter, to walk on every work-day quite across the city from the Via Romana to the Via Martelli, and to the end of the Via del Cocomero (now Via Ricasoli). Our uncle walked with us, and from habit took steps of such great length and velocity that we trotted after him, panting. Occasionally, however, on account of indisposition or business, he had to let us go alone, and then we used to take our revenge. We would walk at our ease, and stop on the Ponte Vecchio to admire the goldsmiths' and jewelers' shops. I won't say that the pastry-cooks' shops did n't attract us too.

When ten years old I felt no leaning to-

ward any vocation. My father's will was
mine; and I do not remember feeling distaste
for any task that was given me. Whatever
was marked out for me to study, it was all the
same to me: history interested me, grammar
attracted me, in arithmetic I found pleasure,
geography amused me, and as to penmanship
and spelling, I had a real passion for them.
Three years later I was just beginning Latin
when my father came to Florence to play for
an entire season. During those three years,
however, my uncle had often taken me to my
father in vacation-time, particularly if he happened to be in a place not far from Florence.
Upon these occasions we would see him play
in the evening, which was to us a source of
unmeasured enjoyment. I took especial delight in dramas and tragedies. When the
company gave a comic piece, I used to ask
my father to let me go to bed.

During one of my vacations, I went alone
with my father to Milan, my brother being ill
with measles, and I had the good fortune to
see a piece played by that wonderful artist
Luigi Vestri. The play was a translation
from the French entitled " Malvina," and for
the first time I learned that one can cry and

laugh at the same time. Vestri, who had been endowed by Nature with all that she can grant to a dramatic artist, made so strong an impression on my boyish imagination, that when my father presented me to him the next day I stared at him as if under a spell, and was unable to utter a word. I fancied that I was in the presence of a divinity. He patted my face kindly, and I felt a wave of delight rush through my veins.

About this time a disaster befell my poor father's household. His second wife, whom in our short visits we had hardly learned to know, unmindful of the sacrifices which her husband had made for her, ungratefully abandoned him. He was so deeply affected that only the thought of his sons restrained him from suicide. For several months he gave himself up to grief, and to projects of vengeance which his good sense and dignity caused to come to naught; and it was after this that he came to Florence for a season, as I have said. I was then thirteen years old; but, strange to say, I looked fully seventeen. So precocious was my development that not only was I a head taller than the tallest of the boys of my age, but my whole figure was in proportion, and I needed only a little hair on my face to have the presence of a young man of twenty. When my father caught sight of me, he exclaimed:

"My goodness! what are you going to grow up to be? The giant Goliath?"

"No, father," I answered; "I prefer to be David, who killed him."

"Well, you shall come with me," said he, "and I will be your Saul in his good moments. If you can't play the harp to charm away the grief of my soul, you can talk to me, and the sound of your voice will soothe me."

Accordingly, when, after the carnival season in Florence, my father joined the Bon and Berlaffa Company as leading actor, he took me with him, leaving my brother to his course at the Fine Arts.

THE AUTHOR'S FIRST APPEARANCE

THE Bon and Berlaffa Company alternated in its repertory between the comedies of Goldoni and the tragedies of Alfieri.

One evening the "Donne Curiose" by Goldoni was to be given, but the actor who was to take the harlequin's part, represented in that piece by a stupid slave called *Pasquino*, fell sick a few hours before the curtain was to rise. The company had been together for a few days only, and it was out of the question to substitute another play. It had been decided to close the theater for that night, when Berlaffa asked:

"'Why could n't your Tom take the part?'"

My father said that there was no reason why he should n't, but that Tom had never appeared in public, and he did n't know whether he had the courage.

The proposition was made to me, and I accepted on the spot, influenced to no little extent by a desire to please the managers, who in my eyes were people of great importance. Within three hours, with my iron memory, I had easily mastered my little part of *Pasquino*, and, putting on the costume of the actor who had fallen ill, I found myself a full-fledged if a new performer. I was to speak in the Venetian dialect; that was inconvenient for me rather than difficult, but at Forte, where we were, any slip of pronunciation would hardly be observed.

It was the first time that I was to go on the stage behind the dazzling footlights, the

first time that I was to speak in an unac-
customed dialect, dressed up in ridiculous
clothes which were not my own; and I confess that I was so much frightened that I
was tempted to run back to my dressing-
room, to take off my costume, and to have
nothing more to do with the play.   But my
father, who was aware of my submissive disposition toward him, with a few words kept
me at my post.

"For shame!" said he; "a man has no right
to be afraid."   A man! I was scarce fourteen,
yet I aspired to that title.

The conscript who is for the first time under fire feels a sense of fear.   Nevertheless,
if he has the pride of his sex, and the dignity
of one who appreciates his duty, he stands
firm, though it be against his will.   So it was
with me when I began my part.   When I
perceived that some of *Pasquino's* lines were
amusing the audience, I took courage, and,
like a little bird making its first flight, I arrived at the goal, and was eager to try again.
As it turned out, my actor's malady grew
worse, so that he was forced to leave the company, and I was chosen to take his place.

I must have had considerable aptitude for

such comic parts as those of stupid servants,
for everywhere that we went I became the
public's Benjamin. I made the people laugh,
and they asked for nothing better. All were
surprised that, young and inexperienced as
I was, I should have so much cleverness of
manner and such sureness of delivery. My
father was more surprised than anybody, for
he had expected far less of my immaturity
and total lack of practice. It is certain that
from that time I began to feel that I was
somebody. I had become useful, or at least
I thought I had, and, as a consequence, in
my manner and bearing I began to affect the
young man more than was fitting in a mere
boy. I sought to figure in the conversation
of grown people, and many a time I had the
pain of seeing my elders smile at my remarks.
It was my great ambition to be allowed to
walk alone in the city streets; my father was
very loath to grant this boon, but he let me
go sometimes, perhaps to get a sample of my
conduct. I don't remember ever doing anything at these times which could have dis-
pleased him; I was particularly careful about
it, since I saw him sad, pensive, and afflicted
owing to the misfortune which had befallen

him, and soon he began to accord me his confidence, which I was most anxious to gain.

A FATHER'S ADVICE

OFTEN he spoke to me of the principles of dramatic art, and of the mission of the artist. He told me that to have the right to call one's self an artist one must add honest work to talent, and he put before me the example of certain actors who had risen to fame, but who were repulsed by society on account of the triviality of their conduct; of others who were brought by dissipation to die in a hospital, blamed by all; and of still others who had fallen so low as to hold out their hands for alms, or to sponge on their comrades and to cozen them out of their money for unmerited subscriptions — all of which things moved me to horror and deep repugnance. It was with good reason that my father was called " Honest Beppo " by his fellows on the stage. The incorruptibility and firmness of principle which he cultivated in me from the time that I grew old enough to understand have been my spur and guide throughout my career, and it is through no merit of my own that I can count myself among those who have won the esteem of society; I attribute all the merit to my father. He was conscientious and honest to a scruple; so much so that of his own free will he sacrificed the natural pride of the dramatic artist, and renounced the well-earned honor of first place in his company to take second place with Gustavo Modena, whose artistic merit he recognized as superior to his own, in order that I might profit by the instruction of that admirable actor and sterling citizen. My father preferred his son's advantage to his own personal profit.

SALVINI JOINS MODENA'S COMPANY

In Lent of the year 1843, in the city of Padua, we joined Modena's company, which was made up almost entirely of players of less than twenty years. Now, to be exact, I shall have to say that in the contract between my father and Gustavo Modena I figured as the bone that is thrown in for good measure; I was to have no salary, but was bound to do whatever was assigned to me by the director, including appearance as a "super" in case of necessity. This was humiliating, after my little triumphs as *Pasquino* the year before; but my father soothed my susceptibility by telling me that all were subjected to the same condition, which was true. I remembered then that egoistical proverb, "An evil shared is half a joy," and my spirits went up a little. My apprehensions vanished entirely when my father said to me that the time had now come to devote myself seriously to the study of my profession; that in future I must exert myself, and that it was only right that the sacrifice he had made should be compensated by my good will and application; and that I should never have a better chance, since the rudiments and the best example of the drama would be exhibited to me by the most distinguished artist of Italy.

I kissed him, and said, "Papa, I will do the best I can." The next day we went to the theater to receive our instructions from the director.

FIRST IMPRESSIONS OF THE GREAT MODENA

To be frank, my first impression of my future master was not wholly favorable. He

looked to me more like a drover than an actor.
He was fat and flabby, his nose was sunk between his cheeks, his walk was heavy, and his
legs had the appearance of elephantiasis.
Nevertheless, his white and beautifully formed
hand, his vivacious, intelligent, and kind eye,
won my sympathy on the spot. His voice,
though nasal, was sonorous, and seemed to
issue not from his lips, but from his ears or his
eyes, or rather from his wide-open nostrils.
As soon as Modena perceived my father, who
in comparison with him looked like a lord,
they squeezed each other's hands and embraced; then Modena turned to me and exclaimed (as was his habit) in his native dialect:
"Oh, what a good David! Well, my lad, is
your mind made up to study?"

"Yes, Signor Maestro," said I.

"No, no," he said; "call me Gustavo; that
is better. And what have you been studying?"

"Harlequin parts, Signor Gustavo," said I.

"Good!" he said; "now you shall study
this speech, and when you know it you shall
say it to me, putting into it all your intelligence and all your soul." It was the speech
of *Egisto* to *Polifonte* in Alfieri's tragedy of
"Merope"; and the same speech had been

given before me to every new member of the company as a test of his vocation for tragedy. The stage gradually filled up with others of the company, who were to rehearse "La Calomnie" of Scribe, in which neither my father nor I was to appear.

While the rehearsal was in progress, and my father was making the acquaintance of the other artists, Modena turned to me and said, "In this comedy you shall do the little Moor for me." I fancied that the little Moor was a part. Alas! he was merely a lay figure, devised to garnish the stage by the Signora Giulia, Modena's wife. I was directed to blacken my face, and to get myself up in Oriental costume to figure as the attendant of one of the personages of the play. This first assignment did not encourage me at all, and my father, seeing my disappointment, whispered in my ear, "Never mind; only study, and you will have no more 'super' work to do." The following day I was the only one who knew *Egisto's* speech perfectly by heart, and I repeated it to my father, who corrected me, and showed me the most salient points, and finally encouraged me by saying, "There, you have it well enough."

The moment of trial came, and by good luck neither my gestures, nor my voice, nor my expression betrayed the violent palpitations due to my emotion. When I got through, Modena exclaimed: " You have some foundation! you 'll make a man for me!" and with this were assigned to me the parts of *Masham* in Scribe's " Un Verre d'Eau"; of *Perez*, *Filippo*, and *Gionata*, in Alfieri's "Saul"; of *Massimiliano Piccolomini* in Schiller's " Wallenstein"; of *Pietro Tasca* in the "Fornaretto" of F. Dall' Ongaro; of the *Lover* in Manzoni's tragedy "Adelchi," and of the lovers in such plays as my father should give on Modena's off-nights. Since I appeared every night, the "super" business troubled me no more. My father had to provide my costumes for all these parts, which was no light expense; but he supported the burden willingly, since he saw the lighting of a fair dawn in the morning of my career. In order to master so many parts in the shortest possible time, I had to sacrifice many hours of sleep. Toward the end of the season, I could have slept on a couch of thorns; and often when my father and I were returning home after supper, and he, becoming interested in some discussion with a friend, ceased to attend to me, my eyes would close, and at the first corner I would lean my head against the wall and fall quietly asleep on my feet. My father, noticing that I was gone, would turn back and take me by the arm, and when we reached home would lay me down on my bed; and the next morning I would wake up and would not know how I got there! What an admirable age youth is! It supports without complaining the inconveniences of life, and adapts itself gladly to every hard condition, if only it is spurred on by ambition. And at fifteen everything looks rose-colored.

My rose was destined soon to change to black. At the end of the year of my novitiate, in Lent of 1844, my father fell ill at Palma Nuova. Just at that time I was burdened more than ever with study, as Carlo Romagnoli had left the company, and all the parts which had been given to him the year before were transferred to me in addition to my own, among them *David* in "Saul," *Nemours* in "Louis XI.," *Luciano* in "La Calomnie." The doctor pronounced my father's malady an inflammation of the bowels, and prescribed frequent baths with bran. In our house the only source of water was a very deep well, and it became my duty to draw water to fill the tub. It was a serious fatigue; but because of the purpose of the task, and perhaps a little because the muscles of my arms began to show a prodigious development from the constant exercise, I was never willing to surrender the charge to others, and performed it regularly for twenty-three days. The company was then about to finish its engagement at Palma Nuova, and my father summoned me to his bedside and told me that I must go on to Cremona with the director, who would be hampered without me. He said that as soon as he was well enough he would follow, but in the mean time it was out of the question to put that excellent man, our director, to loss by depriving him of one of the most important men of his company. I opposed this decision with energy, but I was compelled to yield to my father's repeated commands. I left him in charge of the people of the house, and engaged a man besides to nurse him, and I took my leave of him with tears and kisses. I felt myself sadly alone without my father's accustomed guidance. It is true that he had become still more grave, and was even in-

GUSTAVO MODENA.

clined to misanthropy; but frequently he would forget his troubles in reading to me some extracts from a play he was writing; or in declaiming a bit of Metastasio, his favorite author; or in talking to me of my poor dead mother, whom I never knew, since she died when I was two years old; or of my brother, who was pursuing his studies, or my aunt and uncle, who lived in Florence. One evening at Venice, as we were passing in our gondola before the illuminated Piazzetta di San Marco, he embraced me with silent but profound expression of tenderness, and after a little he said:

"Do you see that lamp burning there before that image? That flame commemorates the unpardonable mistake of the sentence of poor Fornaretto, whose part you play; and that light will not be extinguished so long as man is capable of calling himself infallible."

In my ingenuousness and ignorance I asked, "Papa, how long will that be?"

He smiled, and said: "Ah, my son, that lamp will burn on forever." I felt something like a weight in my soul, and that answer was perhaps the inception in me of the first germs of distrust in my fellow-men.

A GREAT AFFLICTION

My father wrote to me from his sick-bed at
Palma Nuova, exhorting me to behave well,
to be studious, and to be loyal to the wishes
of the director. But I noticed that with every
letter his beautiful handwriting was growing
less firm and even, and I began to fear that
he was becoming much worse. I begged
Gustavo Modena for permission to visit him,
but he refused me absolutely. After a few
days I went to him again, and repeated my
request in a tone of supplication. With a
kinder manner than before he explained to
me in what a dilemma I should put him if I
were to go, as it was entirely impossible for
him to find understudies for my parts; he
said that he should have to close the theater,
which would be at once a dishonor to him and
a very serious loss; and he assured me that
he had had direct news from his friend Beppo,
as he called my father, and that he was de-
cidedly better, and would soon be able to re-
join us. These were fair words, but they did
not reassure me, for no more letters came
from my father. One morning, without saying anything more to Modena, I went to the

police-bureau to reclaim my traveling-permit,
which had been issued in my name when I
was separated from my father; but the Austrian official refused to surrender it without
the consent of the director of my company.
I hurried, beside myself, to Modena, and
said:

"Maestro, I get no more letters from my
father, and I have no news of him. I fear that
something is wrong. Now you will either
give me permission to go to Palma Nuova, or
I will start out on foot and take the risk of
being arrested."

Modena answered very dryly: "What do
you want to go there for? Your father is
dead."

May God pardon him the pain he gave me
at that moment, in return for all the kindness
I had from him at other times! He should
not be judged too harshly; he was tormented
by my persistence, and the obstinacy of my
determination, and by the thought of the consequences to him which must follow, and he
fancied that by that brutal announcement he
would at once deprive me of all hope, put an
end to my plans, and relieve himself from further embarrassment. He took the view that

to so grave an evil should be applied a heroic remedy. I fell to the floor like a log, senseless; and when I came to myself I was in my bed, and my young comrades were by my side, impotent to calm the hysterical spasms which sent me into fit after fit of delirium. For four days I was in bed with aching bones, bruised and sore, and with frequent spells of convulsive sobbing. I learned that during this time my uncle had gone to Palma Nuova and had paid all the last sad offices to the dead; and so at fifteen I was left an orphan, and with the responsibility of working out alone my support and my future.

SALVINI LEAVES MODENA

IT was now necessary for Gustavo Modena to accord me some salary to enable me to live, and I remember that my pay was about fifty cents a day. Sometimes when I was cast for an important part he would give me a dollar as extra compensation; this happened very seldom, but I had enough to live on with careful economy. When we came to Milan, however, three tailors, claiming to be creditors of

my father, presented themselves, and asked
me what were my intentions as to obligations
standing against the name of Giuseppe Salvini.

"My intentions?" said I. "I will pay in
full; I ask only for time." They had three
notes of 1000 francs each, which my poor
father had indorsed for a friend of shaky
credit who had never paid them. The notes
were renewed so that they provided for payment within three years, and I signed them.
The reader can imagine how hard pressed I
felt myself under these obligations, which I
must meet with what economies I could
make from my meager pay. During the remainder of the year I was nevertheless able to
hoard up 300 francs, which I sent in advance
of the time fixed to Lampagnano at Milan,
on account of my debt. With regret, but
constrained by necessity, I sold some of my
father's theatrical wardrobe, and was thus
able to meet all my engagements for that year.

When misfortunes befall, they never come
singly; and of this I was now to have painful
experience. Soon after my father's death an
unlucky incident happened, which compelled
me to sever my connection with Modena. I
had inherited from my father, besides his cos-

tumes, of which I had sold a part, a beautiful
wig of long, golden-blond hair, which he used
to wear as *Charlemagne* in "Adelchi," and
which I wore in the part of *Massimiliano
Piccolomini* in "Wallenstein." After wearing
it, I used to give it in charge of Graziadei, the
hair-dresser of the theater, to put by for me
in a box. One evening Signora Giulia Modena, who occupied herself with much taste
and competence about the dresses of the
artists, asked me to lend her my wig. Now
to me this wig was a most precious possession, both because it came to me from my
father, and because it was to go on my own
head; so I refused her request as civilly as I
could, and no more was said about it. The
next evening I perceived on the head of one
of the "supers" my beloved wig, which the
Signora Giulia had obtained from the hair-
dresser on some trumped-up pretext. With
a "bee in my bonnet" (at that time such bees
were numerous with me), and my wig in my
hand, I presented myself before the Signora,
and made my remonstrance:

"I wish to know, Signora Giulia, who gave
you the right to use my wig, after I told you
that you could n't have it?"

"Come to Gustavo, and you will find out,"
said she to me.

We went to Modena's dressing-room, and I
repeated my demand. Could he in my presence blame his wife, recognize that I was right,
and that she was guilty of an unwarranted
act? Could he, a Modena, my master, make
excuses for her to me, his pupil? He con-
tented himself with saying, "Go, boy; go!"
He did n't put his wife in the wrong, nor did
he admit that I was right; it was no doubt
the best thing he could do. But that word
"boy" cut me to the heart, and I left the room
without a word.

The next day I wrote him a letter notifying
him that from that moment I ceased to belong
to his company, since it was manifest that a
mere "boy" could not be qualified to take the
chief parts after himself. For his answer he
sent to me Massini, the secretary, and some
of the senior members of the company, to
demonstrate to me that it was not making a
very good start in my profession to leave my
company in the middle of the season. My
friends told me further that Signora Giulia
admitted that she had acted arbitrarily, and
that it would be an ungrateful thing on my

part to leave the director in the lurch. This last reason won my consent to remain until the end of the year. Three weeks later I was under contract for the next year with the Royal Company of Florentines in Naples, for first and second lovers' parts, at a salary of 2400 francs. Modena engaged in my place a young man from Leghorn of excellent physical and mental qualities and good artistic promise, Ernesto Rossi by name. He has not disappointed the hopes formed of him in his youth. He, too, guided by the counsels and advice of our master, has gained the esteem of all Italy, and in his tours through Europe and America has done honor to his country.

The six months that I had still to stay with Modena passed in perfect harmony with him and his wife, for both of whom I felt real affection and respect. The nearer came the time when I must leave them, the more fond I grew of them, admiring in her the faithful consort of an exiled citizen, and honoring in him the upright man, the distinguished artist, and the unswerving patriot. Not many days before our separation, I began to realize what a great advantage it had been to me to have his advice, his precepts, his instruction, and his example, and I treasured all these up for the future. When at last we parted, I felt as if I had lost a second father; and I am sure, from his visible emotion, that he felt toward me as if I were his son.

MODENA'S METHOD OF TEACHING

MODENA'S system of instruction was more by practice than by theory. In our day he would be blamed, now that it is considered needful that actors should know everything that has to do in any way with their subjects, no matter how little of it they may be able to put to profit. He rarely spent much time in explaining the character, or demonstrating the philosophy of a part, or in pointing out the reasons for modesty or for the vehemence of passion. He would say, "Do it so," and it would certainly be done in a masterly way. It is true that those pupils who were unable to emancipate themselves, and to act as he told them indeed, but with their own resources and expression of their own feeling, developed into mere imitators. In proof of this it is easy to show that most of Modena's pu-

pils, not excepting some who attained a certain reputation, copied him more in his faults
than in his merits.

ADELAIDE RISTORI

AFTER leaving Modena, I turned my face
toward Naples; but when I came to Leghorn
I learned that I should not have to appear
during Lent, as it was not the custom for new
actors to play until after Easter. I was pleas-
antly settled with some old friends of my
father's, and I determined to wait to see
Adelaide Ristori, who was then playing in
Leghorn, and whom I had never seen.

Ristori was at that time twenty-three, and
had already won most flattering consideration. She was as beautiful as a Raphael Madonna, of graceful figure, attractive, and of
polished and dignified manners. She enjoyed
even then the reputation of being one of the
most youthful and beautiful actresses on the
stage, and at the same time one of the most
gifted; and with good reason rival managers
contended to secure her. She was a pupil of
the noted Carlotta Marchionni, who for many

years was the ornament of the Royal Company of Turin, and held the highest place
among artists of distinction. From Signora
Marchionni Ristori acquired a wealth of practical and theoretical knowledge, and this, with
her essentially artistic nature and her strong
will, made her in a few years the favorite of
the public throughout Italy. Many fell in
love with her, and those who escaped losing
their hearts admired her. Young and ardent,
almost too poetic, as I was, I could not remain indifferent to the unconscious charming
of that siren; and although my heart was already inclined to other sympathies, in presence of Ristori's acting it was invaded by a
sentiment of respectful affection. I remember
that one evening when she played a drama
from the French entitled "La Comtesse d'Al-
temberg," I cried, out and out, during a moving scene in which a mother reproaches her
daughter for suspecting her of being her rival
in love. Though I knew well that my congratulations could have but small weight, I
could not refrain from assuring her of my
warm admiration; and she was kind enough
to appear pleased. But when she said that
she was proud to receive the homage of a

pupil of the reformer of dramatic art, she put so marked and ironical an accent on her words that I remained in doubt whether she was mocking me, or whether she intended to direct a shaft against the renown of Gustavo Modena. I should have preferred the first intention to the second.

ACTING WITH RISTORI — SERVICE UNDER GARIBALDI — ESTIMATE OF RACHEL

AT the age of sixteen I found myself in Naples, a member of the Royal Florentine Company. The older actors of the company were great favorites with the Neapolitans, whose sympathy and liking it is not difficult to gain. I brought with me the modern ideas inculcated by the teaching of my master, Modena, and the fresh influence of Adelaide Ristori. It can be imagined how I felt in the musty, heavy, unhealthful atmosphere to which I had come. I felt like a first officer who was taking the place of a cabin-boy. The only course open to me was to calm my rebellious spirit, to force myself to breathe that atmosphere, the reverse of vivifying though it was, and to keep faithfully

the engagements which I had made. There
were undoubtedly artists of ability in that
company, but their method was antiquated,
except in the case of Adamo Alberti, who
was a most spirited and vivacious comedian ;
moreover, all spoke with the accentuation and
inflections of the Neapolitan dialect, so that
my speech, and that of the other new actors,
contrasted unpleasantly with that of the old
members. The parts that were allotted to
me were of little substance, and I had them
in such aversion that I could not bring myself
to study them; I was discouraged and humiliated to such a degree that the expressions of
displeasure of the public due to my not knowing my lines failed to arouse me from my
apathy. To my professional friends who
sought to encourage me, I said: "The public is perfectly right; but I cannot help it. It
is not possible for me to interest myself in
such colorless and inept parts."

Through the influence of one of the new
actors who sympathized with me, I was cast
for the part of *Annio* in the "Clemenza di
Tito" of Metastasio, and on the night when
I appeared in this part, which was highly
sympathetic to me, I had an enthusiastic re-

ception. The so-called *camorra* (ring) was,
however, so well organized in that musty as-
semblage of artists that I had no chance of
getting many such opportunities to distinguish
myself. The fear of innovation terrified them,
and they were careful to guard against it. I
had engaged with that company for three
years, with annual augmentation of my salary;
but at my earnest request the manager, Signor
Prepiani, canceled my contract from the date
of the ensuing carnival. That year, 1845, was
a most unhappy one for me, abounding in
moral and material sacrifices. Out of my
salary of 2400 francs, I paid 700 to Lampu-
gnani, and 500 on account of the debt of 1000
to Rossi of Brescia. I lived at a boarding-
house, where I paid two francs and a half a
day for my bed and dinner, having for break-
fast a small piece of bread dipped in the juice
of a melon. The remembrance of the important parts which I used to play with my
master, and of the spontaneous and gratifying
favor accorded by the public, was constantly
before me, and the contrast made my new
position seem all the more humiliating. I
grew peevish and rebellious, and secretly
cherished thoughts of revenge. I planned to

return when all the old and moldy material
of that company should have disappeared,
and to put to shame the artists who hoped
for my failure. This plan did not testify to
excessive modesty on my part, but at sixteen
a little vanity is excusable. In the midst of
my justifiable acrimony, I could not but recognize incontestable merits in some of my
opponents. But not one of these actors and
actresses could go outside of the kingdom of
the Two Sicilies without exposing himself or
herself in the theaters of all other Italian
provinces to criticism and censure on account
of the gestures, the accent, and the manner-
isms which they had breathed in with the
Neapolitan air.

In the course of the year that I spent at
Naples, I was enrolled as *primo amoroso* in
the Domeniconi and Coltellini company, to
which were to belong, among other artists of
merit, Carolina Santoni, Antonio Colomberti,
Gaetano Coltellini, and Amilcare Bellotti. In
this new and more sympathetic companionship I breathed more freely, and began to
cultivate with study and application my natural artistic bent, which I had feared to lose
at Naples, but which was merely dormant.

Since I was under engagement to pay the last 1000 francs to the costumer Robotti, brother of the well-known actress, I lived with rigid economy throughout the year 1846 also, when at last my debt was canceled. After that I was able to sleep in peace at night, for I was delivered from the fear of being unable to meet my obligations. The year ran its course for me without great praise or serious discredit; if I was blamed for any shortcoming, it was for nothing more than a certain lack of energy, which was the result of my experience in Naples, and which I could not shake off at once. On the other hand, I soon gained the friendship of the manager and of my associates in the company, who perceived in me, perhaps, some tendency to advance. Coltellini reëngaged me for the following year, with the rank of *primo attore giovane*, and an increased salary, and Domeniconi, who had been absent, resumed the active management. This most intelligent artist had not received from nature the gift of good looks, or of an artistic type of face, or of a natural method, except in comedy; but he had the merit of appreciating and giving expression to the most intimate thoughts of his

3

authors, and that to a degree in which no
other artist could rival him. From Gustavo
Modena and Luigi Domeniconi I acquired
the foundation of my art; and while careful
not to copy the first, and not to ape the manner of the second, I sought to profit by what
I could gain from both.

IN ROME

In the autumn of that year the company
opened at the Teatro Valle in Rome. It was
the first time that I had set foot in the ancient capital of the world; and during my
hours of liberty I visited untiringly its monuments, its galleries, its splendid churches, and
its admirable suburbs abounding in handsome
villas. I believe I formed a just conception
of the greatness of that ancient race which
dominated the world. I found Rome over-
joyed at the famous Encyclical, and at the
liberal principles of the Supreme Pontiff,
whom all proclaimed the savior of his people.
The idolatry of Pius IX. was universal, and
I, like everybody else, paid him the tribute
of my enthusiasm, and used to repeat from

memory sonnets which sang of his saintly
virtues, and heaped maledictions on Austria
as the enemy of every generous aspiration of
Italy. Both the political and the ecclesiastical censure were abolished, and we were free
to give many plays which before had been
on the Index.

AN AUSTRIAN SPY GETS US IN TROUBLE

ONE evening, going casually to the dressing-
room of the first actor, Antonio Colomberti,
I found there a gentleman of distinguished
appearance and somewhat advanced age,
whom I did not know, and who was presented
to me by Colomberti. When we met in the
street afterward, we saluted each other cour-
teously, until one day a Roman friend with
whom I was walking touched my arm, and
asked, "Who is that you are bowing to?" I
answered, "A gentleman who was presented
to me the other night by Colomberti." "Don't
you know," said he, "that that person pre-
tends to belong to the Carbonari association,
and is really a spy on the Targhini and Mon-
tanari, who cannot lift their heads without his

reporting it?   He is a spy paid by Austria!"
After that I turned my head away every time
I met him, and pretended not to see him.
The spy saw through this, and swore vengeance.   A few days afterward I was invited
to a country resort,—a vineyard, as they call
them in Rome,—to be present at a lottery
for which some thousands of people of all
ranks had come together.   In a moment of
enthusiasm, aroused by the political speeches
which had been made, and nourished by co-
pious libations, I was lifted by main force
upon the bottom of an overturned cask, and
called upon to recite some patriotic rhymes.
My success was proclaimed with loud applause.   A son of the spy was present,—an
educated and liberal young man, who was
ignorant of the despicable and infamous trade
of his father,—and when he went home he
told all about the lottery, not forgetting my
success as a reciter of inflammatory verses.
The personage in question, whom out of regard for his son I will not name, caught the
opportunity like a ball on the fly, and sent
such a good recommendation of me to the
Austrian government, that next year, when
I was on my way to Trieste, whither the

rest of the company had preceded me, upon reaching the frontier I was searched and subjected to an examination, and finally the sentence was inscribed upon my passport, "Forbidden to enter the dominions of Austria!" I was in a dilemma. There was nothing for me to do but to recross the Po; and when I reached Ferrara, I wrote to a friend at Bologna, explaining my position, and begging him to send me some money as a loan, for I had nothing. As soon as the money came, my first thought was to relieve my manager Domeniconi from embarrassment, for without me he could not begin his representations; and I resolved, if repulsed at one point, to try again at another. I went to Ancona, destroyed my compromising passport, and from the consul of Tuscany secured a permit to travel which authorized me to proceed from Ancona to Trieste by sea. When I landed in Trieste I was promptly arrested, and conducted under guard to the Imperial and Royal Bureau of Police. They asked me what I meant by my impudence and obstinacy in daring to set foot upon Austrian soil after I had been warned to keep off. I set forth my reasons, and protested that I was a

3*

victim of calumny; and at last, through the intercession of the Countess Von Wimpffen, a friend of Ristori, the concession was made that I might remain in Trieste until orders concerning me could arrive from Vienna. One might have thought that all this fuss was about one of the most dangerous of conspirators. Efforts were made to obtain authorization for me to stay in Venice also, for which place we were booked after leaving Trieste; and I secured permission, under bonds, to fulfil my engagements there with the company, upon condition that I should present myself every day at the police office, "to show myself," as they put it. This requirement became rather a joke, for every morning the consecrated formula would be this: I would say, "Good morning," and the Commissary would answer, "I hope you are well," and I would take myself off.

One evening, rather late, as I was leaving the Caffè Chiodi to return to my lodgings, I noticed on the further side of the Ponte della Verona five persons who were barring the narrow way by which I must pass. The idea of an attack flashed through my brain. I was ashamed to turn back, and besides it was

very cold, and I was anxious to get to bed.
I made the motion of grasping a weapon
under my cloak, and putting on a bold face
I walked resolutely through the suspicious
group. Just as I had passed, I heard one
say to the others, "It is he." I turned on
my heel and demanded, "Whom do you
mean?" The chief stepped forward and said,
"Go on your way, Signor Salvini; as for us,
we are under orders to watch you." "So
much the better," said I; "if that is the case,
I shall be all the safer on my way home."
It would take a volume to tell all the annoy-
ances, the troubles, the persecutions, which
I had to undergo because of that unlucky
introduction of Colomberti's at Rome. I
learned a lesson from it — never to make in-
troductions except between persons who are
well known to me.

ACTING WITH RISTORI

WHAT I have been narrating, as will have
been observed, began in the year 1846 and
extended into the following year; but to omit
nothing of importance, I must now take a step

backward.   In Lent of 1847, I was in Siena
with my new manager, Domeniconi, with Ristori as leading lady, and other actors of
ability.   My new class of parts supplied me
with a task which it was not easy to carry
through: it was customary in Lent to close
the house on Fridays, but on every other
night of the week I had to appear in a new
part, and in company with artists of established
reputation.   O Memory, goddess of my youth,
how great is my debt to thee!   At six in the
morning I used to pass out one of the city
gates with the part I was to play in my hand,
often walking on a thin coating of snow.   I
would walk miles without noticing the distance, and it was my boast that when the
hour of rehearsal came I would make the
prompter's office a sinecure.   All were astonished at me, and the more so because of the
thirty-six new parts which were handed down
to me to learn by the young actor to whose
place I had succeeded, six were in verse.   I
will not seek to deny that I was spurred on
not only by my love for art, but by a softer
sentiment—by my resolution not to be un-
worthy of the affectionate encouragement bestowed upon me by Ristori, for whom I burned

with enthusiasm. But when we came to
Rome, in the spring, I perceived that her
generous and confidential encouragement was
intended not for the young man, but solely for
the young artist! I did not prize it the less
for that, and I continued to love her as a
friend, and to admire her as an artist. I was
seventeen, and my disillusion did not wound
my heart, but enriched my store of experience.
At that time Ristori was my ideal as *Francesca da Rimini*, as *Juliet*, as *Pia di Tolommei*,
and in a host of other rôles in both drama and
comedy, in which she put forth all the per-
fume and freshness of the true in art. All the
gifts and virtues which adorned her as a
woman and as an actress united to influence me to be worthy of her companionship.
Surely, Adelaide Ristori was at that time the
most charming actress in Italy.

FIRST GREAT SUCCESS IN TRAGEDY

THAT year in Rome an incident occurred
which conduced not a little to raise my artistic
reputation in public esteem. Many years before, in that city, the celebrated Lombardi had

played Alfieri's "Oreste." Ventura, Ferri,
Capidoglio, all famed actors, and finally Gustavo Modena himself, had tried it, but had not
succeeded in overcoming the strong impression left by Lombardi, who possessed in profusion the precise requisites for that character — good looks, youth, voice, fire, delivery,
intelligence : so they were enumerated to me,
who had never had the good fortune to see
him. Some years had passed since the last of
the unsuccessful attempts to revive "Oreste,"
when, upon the occasion of a benefit which
was to be given me, I expressed to an old
dilettante who was president of one of the
best philanthropic societies of Rome my desire to appear in that part. The old gentleman, who took much interest in my progress,
exclaimed : "Dear me ! my son, do you want
to tempt fortune, and to play all your future
on one card? Think of what a risk you would
run. Others, more experienced than you,
have tried it, and have been sorry. Don't be
so stubborn as to put yourself in a fair way to
lose all you have gained in the favor of the
public. My son, don't do it."

I was in truth very young, and, like the lava
which pours from a volcano, I knew no ob-

stacles; therefore, for my benefit I imposed
upon the company, as was my right, the
tragedy of "Oreste." The night of the representation came. My ears were tingling with
discouraging warnings; the state of mind I
was in is beyond description; yet I found
some comfort in my own secret reasoning. I
said to myself: "As *Romeo* in 'Giulietta e
Romeo,' as *Paolo* in 'Francesca da Rimini,'
as *Carlo* in 'Filippo,' as *Egisto* in 'Merope,'
I have found favor with the public; why
should I lose it as *Oreste*, a character which
moves me powerfully, and for which I have as
suitable physical gifts as anybody?" I went
to the Teatro Valle three hours before the rising of the curtain; I dressed myself at once,
and went to pacing up and down behind the
scenes like a wild animal, speaking to no one
and answering no one. I overheard my comrades saying among themselves, "Salvinetto
is a fool!" "Salvinetto has gone mad!" and
indeed they had good reason to think so. The
auditorium was soon crowded. The play had
not been given for many years in Rome; the
public was eager to see it again, and was
attracted by the sympathy which my name
enjoyed, and by curiosity to witness a success,

so that not a place in the theater was left
vacant. The first act ended with applause
for Ristori (*Elettra*), for Job (*Clitennestra*),
for Domeniconi (*Egisto*). As I stood behind
the scenes I envied them, and thought of the
hisses which were perhaps about to greet me.
The interlude of music which precedes the
second act ended, and *Oreste* must go on
immediately. My *Pilade* (Giacomo Glech)
said to me, "Courage! Courage!" "I have
it for sale," said I; "do you want some?"
and at once I went on. I made my entry
without speaking, without bowing my thanks
for the applause which attended my appearance; I identified myself absolutely with the
personage whose part I was representing.
After manifesting by gestures my joy upon
recognizing the ancestral scenes from which
Oreste had fled at the age of five, I delivered
my first verse: "Pilade, yes! This is my
realm! O joy!" The public, after the applause of welcome, had resumed silence, eager
to see from the start how that impetuous character would develop itself, and now broke
forth with a roar of approbation which re-
echoed from pit to gallery for as much as two
minutes. Then I said to myself, "Ah! I am

Oreste." As the play went on, and at the end, the applause became enthusiasm. From that moment my title of tragic actor was won, and I was only nineteen!

A CHAPTER OF ACCIDENTS

IN 1848 we made a tour in Sicily. We embarked at Naples, where the political disturbances of that year had not yet manifested themselves. During our stay in Palermo, however, the revolution broke out in the island. Ferdinand II. stopped the steam-packets which communicated with the mainland, and we found ourselves cut off from returning to Rome, where we were bound to appear for a subscription season arranged for by the most distinguished families of the Roman patriciate. Poor Luigi Domeniconi was in despair. He decided to get the whole company together, and proposed that we should charter a brigantine and make the voyage by sail to Civita Vecchia. We accepted on the spot, all the more eager to escape from the trap we were in because we heard that the King of Naples was preparing a strong military expedition for the purpose of invading Sicily and subjugating the rebels. Our provisions were embarked, and we sailed without hindrance out of Palermo on the *Fortunato*, a vessel which had just made a voyage with a cargo of sulphur. We had the lower deck divided into two rooms with canvas, one for the ladies, the other for the men, and laid our mattresses down on the deck, so that the ship looked like a floating hospital. Ristori, who had already become Marchesa Capranica del Grillo, had a sort of state-room of canvas and boards rigged up on deck, and she and her husband were somewhat less uncomfortable than the rest of us. Continuous calms held us back near the Sicilian coast, and the suffocating heat tempted me and some of my friends to plunge overboard into the sea, which was as bright and clear as crystal. We were swimming quietly in the slow wake of our ship, when of a sudden we were startled by a horrified yell. It was the captain, who sprang up on the poop, and called at the top of his voice: "*Santo diavolone!* get on board quick, gentlemen; we are just in the spot where dogfish are most plentiful!" The sailors began to throw morsels of food

as far beyond us as they could, to distract the
attention of the bloodthirsty animals, and in
a twinkling we were again on deck, swarm-
ing up the rope ladder. We got a famous
dressing-down from the captain, who was
responsible for any misfortunes which might
have befallen us as his passengers, and the
experience took away effectually our appetite for swimming.

After four days passed at sea, we had all
come to have prodigious appetites; on the
sixth day our provisions were exhausted, and
we had to get on as best we could with
ship's biscuit and fried potatoes. It occurred
to the cook to make us some fritters of flour
and sugar, which were duly distributed. But
just as we were preparing to swallow with
avidity this unlooked-for dainty, a mighty
yell came from the cook, who had tried one
of his fritters, and with swelled lips and
burning tongue called to us that the fritters
were poisoned! It appears that the cabin-
boy had been sent to the captain's cabin for
the sugar, and had taken by mistake a package of flour poisoned with arsenic for the destruction of rats. Two days more went by,
and from being hungry we became famished.

With the consent of the captain, four of us took the brigantine's boat and rowed off to a fishing-smack to buy the fishermen's catch. But the fishermen declined to sell, saying that they were bound to deliver all they caught to their employer. I explained to them civilly that we had thirty persons on our ship who were actually starving, and that under these circumstances they were not justified in refusing to sell, and I told them that we were willing to pay them twice the value of their fish, but that it was necessary that we should buy them. The blockheads persisted nevertheless in their refusal, and we were obliged to throw courtesy to the winds and to take away a part of their catch by force, for which we threw them a handful of silver. We were pirates, no doubt, but generous pirates. The next morning we made land, and the city of Civita Vecchia gradually came into plain sight. Full of delight, and never doubting that we should sleep that night in good soft beds, we threw our straw ticks overboard; when all of a sudden a violent contrary wind arose, and drove the ship out to sea again. We spent that night on the bare planks of the deck. At last, on the following

RISTORI AS "MARY STUART."

day, we landed at Civita Vecchia, and, weary from our wretched sleeping accommodations, sunburnt, and with throats parched by the heat, we made the best of our way to a *caffè* to get something refreshing. But when we tendered our money to the cashier, he would not take it, because the silver was blackened by the fumes of sulphur, of which the ship was redolent. We all had to set to work to polish our money, and when, after much labor, we had brought the coins back to their original brightness, we succeeded with some trouble in getting them accepted, and were free to set out for Rome. Such a chapter of accidents it all was that some of the company seriously attributed our experience to the presence on the ship of some possessor of the evil eye.

SALVINI ENLISTS

In that year the revolutionary movement assumed extensive proportions. In Rome were gathered all that Italy could boast of honest, liberal, and courageous citizens, lovers of liberty. Pius IX., who had given the first impulse to the progressist and humanitarian theories of the time, became frightened by the menaces of Austria, by the displeasure of the absolute rulers of the other provinces of Italy, and most of all by the insinuations and counsels of the clericals throughout Europe, who hated every aspiration toward liberalism, and he abjured the principles he had professed, and proceeded to Gaeta, to fly from the impetuous wave of the revolution, which would have swept him on into a holy war against the oppressors of Italy. Some time before this, in Rome, as well as in other provinces, the National Guard had been formed, and I had been enrolled in the 8th Roman Battalion.

THE DEFENSE OF ROME

THE republic was proclaimed by the will of the people. Mazzini was one of the three consuls. Among the chiefs of the republican army were Avezzana, Roselli, Garibaldi, and Medici; and the various regiments numbered together about fifteen thousand young men, the flower of the best families of Italy. Louis Napoleon Bonaparte was the President of the

French republic, and to win over the clerical party, which afterward helped him mount his throne, he despatched an expedition which, in conjunction with the forces of the King of Naples, and with the coöperation of a rather shadowy contingent from Spain, had for its objective the reëstablishment of the Pontiff in Rome, and the subjugation of the Italian republicans. As soon as our Triumvirate learned of these projects, it published an edict to the National Guard, summoning all who were in earnest to mobilize for the defense of the walls and fortifications of the city. I and other young artists with me were not the last to report for duty; and soon two battalions of volunteers were ready, under the command of Colonel Masi, who intrusted to us the defense of the walls at the Gardens of the Pope, between the Cavalleggieri and Angelica gates. On April 30 the French, led by General Oudinot, came in sight of Rome, advancing from Civita Vecchia, and were welcomed by a first cannon-shot, which was discharged within ten paces of where I was stationed. I must confess that at that first shot the nerves about my stomach contracted sharply. The French, who were marching in

compact order along the highway, deployed
in skirmishing order in the fields, and opened
a sharp though irregular fire.   On the ram-
parts we had only two small howitzers, and
all about them fell the rifle-balls of the Chas-
seurs de Vincennes, while the French sharp-
shooters were out of range of the bullets of
our muskets.   After covering us with a heavy
fire, they attempted to take our walls by assault; but the hail of balls which we poured
in on them forced them to give up the notion,
leaving the field strewn with their dead and
wounded.

MADE A CORPORAL, AND SET TO BUILDING BARRICADES

ON that same day I was promoted corporal by the commander of my battalion, and
on the night of April 30 I was in charge
of the changing of sentinels, and on the
lookout for a not improbable night assault.
The result of that day had been in our
favor; we had weakened the enemy's ranks
by over 1500, between killed, wounded, and

prisoners. Yet these enemies, too, were republicans, and bore the cock with open wings on their caps, which we saw pierced with our balls when the next morning dawned. For seven days and nights we were not relieved from that post, and our couch was the bare earth. At last we had the good fortune to give over our station to another body of soldiers, but we were at once given the task of constructing barricades at the Porta del Popolo. I had charge of the building of two of them, and these were deemed worthy of praise in the certificate given me in 1861 by General Avezzana, formerly Minister of War. This I am proud to transcribe here, with its note by Garibaldi :

NAPLES, February 12, 1861.

I, the undersigned, attest that Citizen Tommaso Salvini served as a volunteer in the mobilized National Guard posted for the defense of the Vatican Gardens on April 30, 1849, when that position was attacked by the hostile French troops. Further, that the said Salvini, who was subsequently promoted Corporal, continued to serve throughout the siege of Rome, both in the ranks of the Guard and in the construction and defense of barricades, during the whole time of that memorable siege, and that

4*

throughout this time he conducted himself as a warm patriot and a brave soldier.   In testimony whereof I hand to
him the present certificate.

GIUSEPPE AVEZZANA,
General, ex-Minister of War and of Marine.

I recommend to my friend Avezzana our comrade
Salvini.   GIUSEPPE GARIBALDI.

GLIMPSES OF GARIBALDI

AFTER the check of April 30, the French
wanted their revenge, and since they had discovered that our bullets were not made of
butter, and that Italians could fight, two things
which they would never have believed, they
resolved upon a new expedition, this time
of 34,000 men, and with a full siege-train.
During the truce we gave up 300 prisoners,
whom the kind-hearted Italians sent over to
the enemy's camp with their pockets full of
cigars and their stomachs of wine, since they
swore that they had come in ignorance of
the state of affairs, and that they would never
again bear arms against us. When they left
us, they shouted, "*Vive la République Ro-
maine!*" But when our republic had fallen,
we recognized some of them in the hostile

ranks which marched into Rome, with arms in their hands, and the exultation of conquerors on their faces. Our forces dwindled from day to day, and we could not fill the places of the killed and wounded, and of the sick. One day there would be a brush on the Pincio, the next before the Porta Portese, but more often there would be fighting at the Porta San Pancrazio, where I had opportunity to become familiar with the cannon's roar, with the whistling of conical balls, and with the sight of dead and dying, and of mutilation. Behind the stretch of wall which we defended there was a house with a balcony, in which house Garibaldi would often show himself at a garret window to study the movements of the enemy with his field-glass. The front of this house was riddled with French balls, but by a happy fortune none of them ever struck the general, though a young Lombard named Tedeschini, a friend of mine, was hit in the eye by a projectile, and fell from the balcony to the ground. When Garibaldi came out of the house, he saw the poor fellow lying there in his blood, and said, "I told him that this would happen." In point of fact, a short time before he had warned him from his high window of the risk he was running by imprudently exposing his head in a place where he had no cover.

Another day, hearing angry voices at the Porta San Pancrazio, I descended from the gallery where I was posted to see what the trouble was, and I arrived in time to hear a sharp discussion between Garibaldi and Masina. Garibaldi ordered Masina to take his "Knights of Death" and seize the Vascello Casino. Masina observed to the general that there were over 500 French soldiers in that building, and that it was an impossibility for cavalry to dislodge them. Garibaldi retorted:

"If you don't want to go there, I will go."

"No, general," said Masina; "I am going."

He gave the command to his men, but only thirteen mounted their horses to follow him. The San Pancrazio gate was thrown open, and a fruitless hail of balls preceded the sortie of the knights, who charged forth on a full run along the highway toward the Vascello, which was a musket-shot away. In their headlong charge one man fell, pierced by a bullet, but his horse ran on with the others, who rode up the ramp, and in on the lower floor of the Casino. In a moment we heard a repeated and prolonged discharge within, and we saw three of those heroes ride out, and these fortunately regained the gate of Rome unharmed. Masina was not one of them. That must surely have been a very sad day for Garibaldi.

Under the protection of a ditch and a thick hedge along the highway, we advanced from the small postern, under the fire of the French, to retake the bodies and carry them back to Rome. We succeeded, not without difficulty and danger, and were warmly praised by our fellows in arms. Masina's body was unrecognizable, for the French, seeking to prevent us from getting possession of it, had concentrated their fire on his head as he lay a corpse.

THE FALL OF ROME

THE solution of the glorious drama was near. The trenches and rifle-pits planned by the French chief of engineers, Le Vaillant, were completed, the siege-ordnance was placed in position, and shells rained on Rome regularly every five minutes, day and night. Yet the republicans would not capitulate.

It was a heroic protest rather than a defense.
We all knew that we could not hold out
against forces so overwhelming, but we knew
too that there were in Italy generous hearts
full of revolt against the yoke of despotism and tyranny.   The French made seven
breaches in the walls, with the view of securing possession of the heights, and these they
occupied by night, with the aid of traitors, but
not without an obstinate and heroic resis-
tance.   The republic fell, but not the republicans.   As soon as the French had secured
possession of a few important strategic points
in the city, Garibaldi marched out of the
gate of St. John with a few hundred men;
many others left Rome singly, and still more
withdrew quietly to their own houses, filled
with anxiety for the future.   A military proc-
lamation was issued, commanding all persons
to retire to their lodgings at the firing of a
gun every evening at nine o'clock.   Numerous patrols passed through the streets after
that hour.   I, with Missori (who was afterward colonel with Garibaldi, whose life he
saved at Calata Fimi), the professor of music
Dall' Agata, and others who lived in the same
house, used to mock the French patrols, as

they passed under our windows, by imitating the cock's crow at them. After a few days it occurred to me that I might be exposed to some annoyance after the reëstablishment of ecclesiastical rule, and I determined to leave Rome for a time, giving as a pretext my desire to see my relatives, as well as a certain pretty girl to whom I had been attentive for some time. Accordingly I set out from Rome, and embarked at Civita Vecchia on the steamer *Il Corriere Corso* with many emigrants of my acquaintance, among them Aurelio Saffi, Saliceti, Dall' Ongaro, and Sala of Milan. When the steamer put in at Leghorn, where we were to land, the restored government of the Grand Duke refused to receive us, and despatched us on to Genoa. There we found in the port the steamer *Lombardo*, which had taken a large number of the politically compromised, among them Prince Canino Bonaparte, who had been vice-president of the Roman assembly. Our ship was promptly surrounded, like the other, by gunboats; and after lying there three days, we were taken to the Lazaretto della Foce. To those of us who could afford to pay was assigned a room with straw beds on the floor; but the greater

number were forced to remain in the corridors of the establishment. I was in a room
with my friends.

An aunt of mine, who was at Genoa, begged
my liberty of General La Marmora, who was
then commandant of the place, and I was thus
able to leave prison sooner than the rest. I
was impatient to get to Florence, and I presented myself with my passport to the Tuscan
consul, to obtain the necessary *visa*, and then
hurried on board of a packet which was just
sailing for Leghorn. That night the gods
had a famous battle among themselves. It
thundered, it lightened, terrific bolts flashed
down from the heavens, and the wind piled
up the waves in mountains, up which we
crawled only to fall into the abyss beyond.
It seemed as if our nutshell of a steamer must
go to pieces at any moment. A gruesome
noise arose from the dashing about of furniture, the crashing of dishes, bottles, and
glasses, the groaning of the timbers, the
shrieks of some of the women, and the crying of terrified children. The cabin doors
were fastened, but I stayed on deck to enjoy
this grand spectacle of nature; I was obliged
for safety to have myself secured to a mast,

or I should have been washed overboard by
the waves, which broke on deck without in-
termission. In the midst of the disturbance
I fell asleep, and at dawn I was not sorry to
find myself in sight of Leghorn—but in what
a state! I was drenched by the sea and the
steady downpour; I was literally swimming
in my boots, and I had to go to my state-room
and change my clothes from head to foot.

IN PRISON

Upon landing at Leghorn, my first care
was to go to the police bureau for my passport, which I had had to give to the purser
of the steamer before sailing from Genoa.
The chief of police put an infinity of questions to me, and I gave him straightforward
answers, the result of which was that I was
conducted between two gendarmes to the
Lazaretto of St. Leopold, which was at that
time set aside for the detention of political
prisoners. I was put into a large cell with
several young men of Leghorn whom I knew
to be of advanced opinions, and with a supply
of cigars and some bottles of good wine we

spent three days without incident. On the
fourth day I was notified that as my domicile
was in Florence, I must proceed to that city.
Two new guardian angels bore me company
in a coach to the railway station, and were
civil enough to spare me the mortification of
appearing to be under arrest by sitting at
some distance from me in the compartment,
though they were careful not to take their
eyes off me. At Florence another coach was
in waiting, and set me down at the office of
the Commissary of the quarter of San Marco.
It was dinner-time, and all the officials were
out. While I was waiting I discovered a ser-
geant, an ex-dramatic artist, whom I knew,
and I begged him to inform my uncle of my
arrival in Florence as a prisoner. After a
time the officer in charge came in, and, learning that I was domiciled in the Santo Spirito
quarter, he sent me on to the Commissary of
that subdivision of the city. This personage
said, with a most impertinent and offensive
manner, "You look like a very suspicious
character." "You don't mean to say so,"
said I; "that shows that appearances are
deceptive, for, on the contrary, I am the most
amiable young man in the world." This

flighty jack-in-office proceeded to put me through such a tiresome maze of questions that I thought he would end by asking me the name of the priest who baptized me, or that of the barber who gave me my first shave. Just as at Leghorn, the result of all this prying and inquisitorial insinuation was an order to take me to prison.

After five days my uncle came and announced to me that I was at liberty, but under the condition that I should leave Florence at once. My director, Domeniconi, had obtained permission to resume his representations, and wrote me to return to Rome at once, and that he would see to it that I should have nothing to fear from the pontifical police.

BACK IN ROME

But what a Rome it was to which I came back! It was black, barren, lugubrious; characterized especially by the red of the French trousers, and the black of priests' vestments. The few citizens whom one met in the streets looked so sad that one's heart yearned for

them. Those days were gone when all was
life; when the cheerful colors of the nation
adorned the streets, the palaces, the houses,
and even the sunlight seemed brighter for
their presence. Where were all those merry
faces, full of hope, eager for glory and for liberty? Where was that sentiment of kinship
and of equality which made one say when he
met a youth, "He is my brother!" and inspired a filial feeling to every elderly man?
The air had become heavy, the walls gloomy,
the people melancholy; if we met a French
soldier, we said, "There is an oppressor";
if a priest, "There is an enemy of our country." Unhappy Rome! Unhappy Italy!
And with those two exclamations I turned
back to art, the one resource which lay open to
my bruised spirit, and to art I dedicated myself without reserve. I understood perfectly
that the priestly government looked upon me
with an evil eye, and I thought it prudent to
hold myself in complete isolation — all the
more so after I had met Monsignor Mattencei,
governor of Rome, escorted by police agents
in disguise, and he had said to me as he passed,
"Prudence, my young fellow!" I well understood the covert threat, and I spent every

hour that the theater did not require of me in reading and studying in my rooms.

Doubtless it would not be possible for me now to remember how much and what I read during the two years that I continued after this with the Roman company. I was by nature more inclined to poetry than prose, and I gave most of my time to the perusal of the classics in poetry and the drama. Homer, Ossian, Dante, Tasso, Ariosto, Petrarch—the sovereign poets — were my favorites; Metastasio, Alfieri, Goldoni, Nota, Kotzebue, Arelloni, ranked next; and after these my preference was given to the foreign authors — Milton, Goethe, Schiller, Byron, Corneille, Racine, Molière. For the *bonne bouche* I reserved Ugo Foscolo, Leopardi, Manzoni, Monti, and Niccolini.

By familiarizing myself with these great writers, I formed a fund of information which was of the greatest assistance to me in the pursuit of my profession. I made comparisons between the heroes of ancient Greece and those of Celtic races; I paralleled the great men of Rome with those of the middle ages; and I studied their characters, their passions, their manners, their tendencies, to such pur-

5

pose that when I had occasion to impersonate
one of those types I was able to study it in its
native atmosphere. I sought to live with my
personage, and then to represent him as my
imagination pictured him. The nice decision
as to whether I was always right must rest
with the public. It is very certain that to accomplish anything in art requires assiduous
application, unwearied study, continuous ob-
servation, and, in addition to all that, natural
aptitude. Many artists who have ability, eru-
dition, and perseverance will nevertheless
sometimes fall short of their ideal. It may
happen that they lack the physical qualities
demanded by the part, or that the voice cannot bend itself to certain modulations, or that
the personality is incompatible with the character represented.

ABSURDITIES OF THE CENSORSHIP

Our company reopened, then, at the Teatro Valle of Rome, and took the name of
that city. The laws of political and ecclesiastical censure had come again into force, and
we actors had to contend with very serious

difficulties in observing the innumerable erasures and the ridiculous substitutions which the censors made in our lines. The words "God," "Redeemer," "Madonna," "angel," "saint," "pontiff," "purple," "monsignor," "priest," were forbidden. "Religion," "republic," "unity," "French," "Jesuit," "Tartuffe," "foreigner," "patriot," were equally in the Index. The colors green, white, and red were prohibited; yellow and black and yellow and white were also forbidden. Flowers thrown on the stage must not show any of those colors prominently, and if it chanced that one actress had white and green in her dress, another who wore red ribbon must not come near her. If we transgressed we were not punished with simple warnings, but with so many days of arrest, and with fines which varied in amount according to the gravity of the offense. I remember well that one night when I played the *Captain* in Goldoni's "Sposa Sagace" I was fined ten scudi for wearing a blue uniform with red facings and white ornaments, for the excellent reason that the blue looked green by artificial light.

Another time our leading actress was playing *Marie Stuart*, and had to receive the

dying *David Rizzio* in her arms, and to kiss
him on the forehead just as he drew his last
breath. I had to pay twenty scudi for the
kiss I had received without being aware of it!
The priests plainly knew their own minds,
and they did not falter in chastising the err-
ing. The reader can well imagine the effect
upon art of all this interference, and annoyance, and torment. Art, indeed, was treated
as a culprit. Nevertheless, the public continued to fill our house, to applaud, and to be
entertained; and it had then a much truer
feeling for artistic beauty than it has to-day.
The artists, too, were then animated in the
highest degree with the honor that should be
paid to a profession which, whatever else
may be said of it, is eminently instructive
and improving.

HOW THE AUTHOR STUDIED HIS ART

THE parts in which I won the most sympathy from the Italian public were those of
Oreste in the tragedy of that name, *Egisto*
in "Merope," *Romeo* in "Giulietta e Romeo,"
Paolo in "Francesca da Rimini," *Rinaldo* in

"Pia di Tolommei," *Lord Bonfield* in "Pamela," *Domingo* in the "Suonatrice d'Arpa," and *Gian Galeazzo* in "Lodovico il Moro." In all these my success was more pronounced than in other parts, and I received flattering marks of approval. I did not reflect, at that time, of how great assistance to me it was to be constantly surrounded by first-rate artists; but I soon came to feel that an atmosphere untainted by poisonous microbes promotes unoppressed respiration, and that in such an atmosphere soul and body maintain themselves healthy and vigorous. I observed frequently in the "scratch" companies which played in the theaters of second rank young men and women who showed very notable artistic aptitude, but who, for lack of cultivation and guidance, ran to extravagance, over-emphasis, and exaggeration. Up to that time, while I had a clear appreciation of the reasons for recognizing defects in others, I did not know how to correct my own; on the other hand, I recognized that the applause accorded me was intended as an encouragement more than as a tribute which I had earned. From a youth of pleasing qualities (for the moment I quell my mod-

5*

esty), with good features, full of fire and
enthusiasm, with a harmonious and powerful
voice, and with good intellectual faculties, the
public deemed that an artist should develop
who would distinguish himself, and perhaps
attain eminence in the records of Italian art;
and for this reason it sought to encourage
me, and to apply the spur to my pride by
manifesting its feeling of sympathy. By
good fortune, I had enough conscience and
good sense to receive this homage at its just
value. I felt the need of studying, not books
alone, but men and things, vice and virtue,
love and hate, humility and haughtiness,
gentleness and cruelty, folly and wisdom,
poverty and opulence, avarice and lavishness,
long-suffering and vengeance—in short, all
the passions for good and evil which have
root in human nature. I needed to study
out the manner of rendering these passions
in accordance with the race of the men in
whom they were exhibited, in accordance
with their special customs, principles, and
education; I needed to form a conception of
the movement, the manner, the expressions
of face and voice characteristic of all these
cases; I must learn by intuition to grasp the

characters of fiction, and by study to repro-
duce those of history with semblance of truth,
seeking to give to every one a personality
distinct from every other. In fine, I must
become capable of identifying myself with
one or another personage to such an extent
as to lead the audience into the illusion that
the real personage, and not a copy, is before
them. It would then remain to learn the
mechanism of my art; that is, to choose the
salient points and to bring them out, to cal-
culate the effects and keep them in proportion with the unfolding of the plot, to avoid
monotony in intonation and repetition in accentuation, to insure precision and distinctness in pronunciation, the proper distribution
of respiration, and incisiveness of delivery.
I must study; study again; study always.
It was not an easy thing to put these precepts in practice. Very often I forgot them,
carried away by excitement, or by the su-
perabundance of my vocal powers; indeed,
until I had reached an age of calmer reflection I was never able to get my artistic
chronometer perfectly regulated; it would
always gain a few minutes every twenty-four
hours.

In the spring of 1851, Ristori entered the
Royal Company of Turin, while I remained
with Domeniconi that year and until the beginning of 1853. During those two years
our leading lady was Amalia Fumagalli, a
painstaking actress, whose comic face and in-
elegant figure were drawbacks to her — compensated, however, by a sweet voice, a most
moving rendering of emotion, a dexterity that
was beyond belief, and a most uncommon
degree of artistic intuition. If Amalia Fumagalli had been beautiful, she would undoubtedly have rivaled the best actresses of the
day, and particularly so in comedy. In many
parts she certainly ranked first; and especially in Scribe's "Valérie," in "Birichino
di Parigi," and in "Maria Giovanna" she was
inimitable. Debarred as she was by Nature
from that gift which for a woman has most
charm, she had the power to win the esteem
and affection of the Italian public.

RACHEL

At this time I had the fortune to be present at a few representations given by Rachel

at the Teatro Metastasio in Rome. Her name had been preceded by her fame, a thing which is sometimes of assistance to an artist, while it increases greatly his responsibility, and as often is positively harmful. But this was not so with Rachel. What can I say of that incomparable French actress? She was the very quintessence of the art of Roscius; to render due praise to her qualities of mind, as well as to those of face and form, it would be necessary to coin new epithets in the Italian tongue. Expression, attitude, the mobile restraint of her features, grace, dignity, affection, passion, majesty — all in her was nature itself. Her eyes, like two black carbuncles, and her magnificent raven hair, added splendor to a face full of life and feeling. When she was silent she seemed almost more eloquent than when she spoke. Her voice, at once sympathetic, harmonious, and full of variety, expressed the various passions with correct intonation and exemplary measure. Her motions were always statuesque, and never seemed studied. If Rachel had been able to free herself in her delivery from the cadence traditional in the Conservatoire, where she had studied,—a cadence which, it is true, cropped out but rarely,—she would, in my belief, have been perfect. She was the very incarnation of Tragedy. The monotony of the rhyming Alexandrine verses was not suitable to her gifts; she should not have been compelled to speak an impoverished, nasal, uneven, unmelodious language like the French, but the sonorous measures of ancient Greece and Rome.

Was it in her nature or in her art? Both were so completely harmonized in her by genius as to form a new Melpomene. France, who most laudably pays honor to her distinguished children, should not have shared in the unjust war made upon Rachel by certain authors and journalists under the contemptible promptings of spite and ill temper, by leaving that luminous star unheeded to quench itself by inches in languor and melancholy. Her merit was so supreme that we can well pardon some slight defects in her character—defects which were, perhaps, due to the malady which was secretly preying upon her; and both as a woman, and as one who was a real honor to her country, she had the right to expect more indulgence and higher regard from the proverbial equity and courtesy of the French people. The thought that she was disliked by her compatriots exacerbated the disease which brought her to the grave. Poor Rachel! May the compassion of an Italian artist reach you in your eternal abiding-place!

FIRST STUDY OF SHAKSPERE

I REMAINED with Domeniconi for two years after Ristori left us, and during this period I busied myself with reading the works of Shakspere, translated into Italian verse by Giulio Carcano. Although the name of Shakspere had already more than once attracted my attention, the dubious outcome of the experiments of several meritorious artists who had made essay of him had dissuaded me from occupying myself overmuch with his plays.

At that time the quality of form appeared so important to me, that Voltaire seemed to be more acceptable than Shakspere, and I preferred *Orosmane* in " Zaïre " to the *Moor of Venice*. The haughty and impassioned sultan possessed me heart and soul, and I

awaited with impatience the opportunity to
portray him. The character appealed to me
so strongly that I could not get it out of my
thoughts, and it kept fusing itself with the
various new parts for which I was cast by
my director. I already had by heart some
portions of *Orosmane's* lines, and I took pleasure in declaiming them before a mirror, with
a towel wrapped round my head in lieu of a
turban ; and at the start I found some effects
which, as I thought, presaged a sure success.
I wished, however, to avoid fixing an imma-
ture conception in my mind, and I let it lie
for several months, so that I might form fresh
impressions upon taking it up again. There
is no better rule in art than not to permit
one's self to be carried away by a first impulse. When time is taken for reflection,
one's conceptions are always more correct.

It was my aim to form a repertory of special parts so minutely studied and rounded
that I might be able through them to attain
a reputation.

The conditions of the Italian stage at that
time were not such as to offer me the means
of attaining my end. Constrained as I was
to busy myself with a new part every week,

which, though often I did not know the text perfectly, I had to play without reflection, and without having a thorough grasp of it, how was it possible for me to prosecute a serious study of the philosophy and psychology of my art? I resolved to accept no engagement for the coming year (1853), and to live quietly with my relatives in Florence with a view to carry out my plan.

Just then the works of Shakspere came again into my hands, and, to tell the truth, even on a second reading, his characters, his conceptions, and his form seemed to me so strange that I was still in doubt whether to occupy myself with them. Nevertheless, the impression that I received was a strong one, since I was unable to drive from my mind the adventures of the sad, perplexed, and anguish-driven *Hamlet*, and of the loyal, generous, and trusting *Othello*. I made up my mind that I would spend my time, during the next year, on no more than three parts. These were *Saul* and *Othello* in the tragedies of the same names by Alfieri and Shakspere, and *Orosmane* in Voltaire's "Zaïre," which last I had already gotten into pretty good shape. With the carnival of 1853 ended in Bologna my engagement with Domeniconi; but I had to stay through Lent in that city to play at a match in billiards which I had begun during the season. During Lent the Zannoni Company came to the Corso Theater in Bologna, and with a view to bettering their somewhat languishing fortunes, made me a proposal that I should appear in a few extra performances. As I was on the spot, I accepted the proposition, a little out of vanity, and a little for the sake of laying up a few more scudi for the needs of my coming period of leisure. One of the most promising plays to give was undoubtedly "Zaïre"; but I was not a little awed by the fame, still bright in that city, won as *Orosmane* by the celebrated Lombardi. Lombardi must surely have been an artist of great merit to establish himself so firmly in the popular memory. "He who is afraid goes not to the wars," said I to myself, and I decided to seize the chance to give the play. I began my series with "Orestes," "Der Spieler," by Iffland, "Orlando Furioso," and Scribe's "La Calomnie." I did not possess the costumes for *Orosmane*, but with my receipts from the first plays I was able to fit myself out with dresses at once rich and elegant.

On the appointed evening the expectation of the audience was wrought up to a high pitch. Nevertheless, it was favorably disposed; and notwithstanding that in the last act my wide Turkish trousers were awkwardly disarranged precisely at the culminating moment of the tragedy, it was a splendid success. Thus one of the three parts in which I had determined to attain superiority had already received its consecration.

I settled myself very comfortably with my relatives in Florence, and laid out my hours, —so many for study and so many for recreation,— keeping myself free from everything which might disturb my plans. During my frequent walks I declaimed my parts mentally; but now and then I would forget myself, and instantly would become an object of public curiosity. Again I would be surprised by some passer-by in the act of practising a gesture appropriate to the personage who was occupying my mind, and I doubt not that I was often taken for a lunatic. Very often I would seek out-of-the-way and solitary places, pushing on into a fir wood or a chestnut grove, where my only audience would be the birds. A gentleman of Ferrara, who was

fond of declamation, having asked me to give
him lessons, I taught him *Saul*, and took the
opportunity to study it myself at the same
time.   This was the only part in my master's
repertory of tragedy which I ventured to play,
and in the proper place I will explain why.
I avoided the others, fearing lest I should follow him too closely or do less well.   Those
actors whom I saw devote themselves to re-
producing those parts awoke my disgust or
moved me to ridicule; and when sometimes
I heard them applauded by a forgetful or ignorant public, I became indignant, and would
gladly have protested.   I shall always congratulate myself upon my decision to free
myself for that year from the monotonous
routine of the stage.   I gained in this way
the opportunity to reflect, to make comparisons, and to examine into my defects.   I imposed upon myself a new method of study.
While I was busying myself with the part of
Saul, I read and re-read the Bible, so as to
become impregnated with the appropriate sentiments, manners, and local color.   When I
took up *Othello*, I pored over the history of
the Venetian Republic and that of the Moor-
ish invasion of Spain; I studied the passions

SALVINI AS "ICILIO" IN THE "VIRGINIE" OF ALFIERI.

of the Moors, their art of war, their religious
beliefs, nor did I overlook the romance of
Giraldi Cinthio, in order the better to master
that sublime character.   I did not concern
myself about a superficial study of the words,
or of some point of scenic effect, or of greater
or less accentuation of certain phrases with a
view to win passing applause; a vaster horizon opened out before me—an infinite sea on
which my bark could navigate in security,
without fear of falling in with reefs.

FAULTS IN ACTING

In my assiduous reading of the classics,
the chief places were held among the Greeks
by the masculine and noble figures of Hector,
Achilles, Theseus, Œdipus; among the Scots
by Trenmor, Fingal, Cuchullin; and among
the Romans by Cæsar, Brutus, Titus, and
Cato.   These characters influenced me to
incline toward a somewhat bombastic system
of gesticulation and a turgid delivery.   My
anxiety to enter to the utmost into the conceptions of my authors, and to interpret them
clearly, disposed me to exaggerate the modu-

6

lations of my voice like some mechanism
which responds to every touch, not reflecting
that the abuse of this effort would bring me
too near to song.   Precipitation in delivery,
too, which when carried too far destroys all
distinctness and incisiveness, was due to my
very high impressionability, and the straining
after technical scenic effects.   Thus, extreme
vehemence in anger would excite me to the
point of forgetting the fiction, and cause me
to commit involuntarily lamentable outbursts.
Hence I applied myself to overcome the
tendency to singsong in my voice, the exuberance of my rendering of passion, the
exclamatory quality of my phrasing, the precipitation of my pronunciation, and the swag-
ger of my motions.

I shall be asked how the public could abide
me, with all these defects; and I answer that
the defects, though numerous, were so little
prominent that they passed unobserved by
the mass of the public, which always views
broadly, and could be detected only by the
acute and searching eye of the intelligent
critic.   I make no pretense that I was able to
correct myself all at once.   Sometimes my
impetuosity would carry me away, and not

until I had come to mature age was I able to free myself to any extent from this failing. Then I confirmed myself in my opinion that the applause of the public is not all refined gold, and I became able to separate the gold from the dross in the crucible of intelligence. How many on the stage are content with the dross!

THE DESIRE TO EXCEL IN EVERYTHING

My desire to improve in my art had its origin in an instinctive impulse to rise above mediocrity—an instinct that must have been born in me, since, when still a little boy, I used to put forth all my energies to eclipse what I saw accomplished by my companions of like age. When I was sixteen, and at Naples, there were in the boarding-house, at two francs and a half a day, two young men who were studying music and singing, and to surpass them in their own field I practised the scales until I could take B natural. Later on, when the tone of my voice had lowered to the barytone, impelled always by my desire to accomplish something, I took lessons in music from the *maestro* Terziani, and appeared at a benefit with the famous tenor Boucardé, and Signora Monti, the soprano, and sang in a duet from "Belisario," the aria from "Maria di Rohan," and "La Settimana d'Amore," by Niccolai; and I venture to say that I was not third best in that triad. But I recognized that singing and declamation were incompatible pursuits, since the method of producing the voice is totally different, and they must therefore be mutually harmful. Financially, I was not in a condition to be free to choose between the two careers, and I persevered of necessity in the dramatic profession. Whether my choice was for the best I do not know; it is certain that if my success had been in proportion to my love of music, and I have reason to believe that it might have been, I should not have remained in obscurity.

My organization was well suited, too, for success in many bodily exercises. When I wanted to learn to swim, I jumped from a height into the sea out of my depth, and soon became a swimmer; I took a fancy to dancing, and perfected myself to such good purpose that I was always in favor as a part-

ner; I wanted to be a good swordsman, and
for five years I handled the foils assiduously,
and took part in public exhibitions for the
benefit of my teachers. In like manner I
became one of the best billiard-players in
Italy, and so good a horseman that no horse
could unseat me. My muscular strength,
fostered by constant exercise, was such that
with one arm I could lift a man seated in a
chair and place him on a billiard-table. I
could sew and embroider, and make any quantity of pretty little trifles, and I used to devise
new games that gave pleasure to numbers of
my friends. Everything that I tried succeeded
at least moderately well, not from any personal
merit of my own, but owing to the happy
disposition conferred upon me by nature.

As to my character, I must confess that
I was somewhat positive. I was extremely
high-strung, and took offense at an equivocal
word or a dubious look. Though apparently
self-controlled, I was very violent when my
anger was awakened. I was patient in a
very high degree, but firm and resolute in
my decisions. I was constant when once my
affection was seriously given, but changeable
in my sympathies. Friendship was a religion

for me, and notwithstanding frequent decep-
tions, I have always remained an affectionate
friend. Titles of nobility have never dazzled
me; I have always admired the true gentleman, and venerated the man of real talent.
The sentiment of revenge never developed in
me, but that of contempt assumed great proportions. I have never felt envy of any one,
but I have sought to emulate those I have
admired. I have sought for money, not for
the sake of riches, but as a means of independence. I have done much good to my
fellows, and have received evil in return. I
have thought much for others, and have made
little provision for myself; in that little I include the leaden case destined to receive my
bones.

THE CHOLERA IN BOLOGNA

In 1854 I became a member of the Astolfi company, of which Carolina Santoni
was leading lady, and Gaspare Pieri the
brillante. Carolina Santoni had a disagree-
ment with our manager, Astolfi, and left the
company in the middle of the year; her place
was supplied by Gaspare Pieri's wife, the

charming Giuseppina Casali-Pieri, who had some talent in comedy.

We went to Bologna just as the cholera was beginning to appear there; it was threatening at the same time several other cities in Italy. I advised all to leave Bologna at once, and to go to some place that was free from infection; but neither manager nor company would accept my advice, being unwilling to incur the unforeseen expense of a new journey. To mask their stinginess, they declared that my advice was dictated by fear, and Astolfi diverted himself hugely at my expense, and ridiculed the timidity of my proposition. In the mean time the disease was becoming more and more serious, and one day when I saw an expression of grave anxiety on the faces of my late opponents, I said to them: "You refused my advice, and said that it was due to my being afraid. Now all I have to say to you is that I shall be the last of us all to leave Bologna." Soon the victims of the pestilence numbered 500 a day. The city was in consternation, and business was forgotten or neglected. At many street-corners temporary altars were set up, and the people would kneel down before them and pray, and seek to conjure away the danger. One night I myself stumbled over the body of a person who had been suddenly stricken down. In a short time the city became a desert, and only then did my companions decide to go away. They hired carriages by the day to make the journey; and when they had all gone, I took a place in the public coach, and reached Leghorn before them. Our manager, Astolfi, upon his arrival at Pistoja, was taken with the epidemic, and lost his life.

I received a most advantageous offer for 1856 from the jovial and courteous, but none the less able, actor and manager, Cesare Dondini. After Luigi Vestri, this actor was the most faithful follower of the school of truth. The very sight of him put one in good humor; the geniality of his disposition even influenced the audience, and made everybody in the house feel happy, no matter how diverse were the parts which he played. He was a very pearl of a man, and a model manager.

A most brilliant comet was just then rising on the artistic horizon. Clementina Cazzola was born under the patronage of art; as a little girl she was called an infant prodigy. She was the child of artists of humble rank,

but nature had endowed her with the sentiment of the beautiful; and as the workman
extracts the carbuncle from the rock, so did
Cesare Dondini raise from obscurity that
precious gem of the purest water. Her interpretation of her characters was faithful
and exquisitely subtle, and the most minute
analysis of every profound emotion was rendered by her with exactness and truth. Her
eyes were like two black diamonds emitting
beams of light, and seemed quickly to penetrate to the very soul of him upon whom she
fixed them, and to read his inmost thoughts.
In the "Dame aux Camélias" she was be-
witching; in the tragedy of "Saffo," by Ma-
renco, she was admirable; in "Pia de Tolommei" she was sublime. In this last tragedy,
especially, she reached such a pitch of perfection that it seemed a miracle. I am most
happy to render to this incomparable actress
a small part of that homage which the Italian
public lavished upon her. We all deplored
her early death in July, 1858.

While I was still with the Dondini company, the distinguished tragic poet G. B.
Niccolini intrusted to me the production of
his "Œdipus at Colonos," and it met every-

where with a favorable reception.   Other
works, more or less worthy, came at this
time to distract my attention from the studies
of my choice; but these transient interrup-
tions really contributed to ripen those studies.
I could not deviate from my purpose to form
a special repertory for myself, and I had
already made a beginning with " Zaïre," the
"Suonatrice d'Arpa," "Oreste," "Saul," and
my study of "Othello."

OTHELLO

THIS last play I was able to put on the
stage at Vicenza in June, 1856, with Clementina Cazzola as the most perfect type of *Desdemona* that could ever be wished for.   The
usual conception of *Desdemona* is as a blonde,
with blue eyes and a rosy complexion,—perhaps because in his pictures Titian preferred
that type, and cultivated variety in his colors
and half-tints,—but for all that, it is not less
true that the Venetian type is represented by
dark eyes, black hair, and skin of alabaster.
In Venice ruddy-haired women are no more
usual than those with jet-black hair in Eng-

land. That excellent artist, Lorenzo Piccinini, filled most adequately the part of *Iago*.
The material of the company was excellent;
every care had been taken with the costumes,
which were faultless; suitable scenery had
been prepared by a scene-painter of ability,
and the production of Shakspere's play was
awaited with lively interest. It was the night
of my benefit, and abundant and prolonged
applause was given in greeting to the artist;
but it was the first time that a tragedy of that
type had been seen in Vicenza; hence popular judgment wavered as to the worth of the
work. It would be unfair to lay this too
heavily to the charge of a public accustomed
to the observance of the Aristotelian limits
of classic tragedy. It is not the little band
of intelligent persons that we have to convince, but the mass of the public.

From Vicenza we went to Venice, and our
rendering of "Othello" met with the same
reception there. There was applause, there
were calls before the curtain, an ovation even;
but the people, as they left the house, said,
"This is not the kind of thing for us." While
that pale imitation, Voltaire's "Zaïre," was
lauded to the skies, thanks to its irreproach-

able form, "Othello" did not appeal to the
taste of the Venetians.   It will easily be believed that I made little account of this mistaken judgment, and repeated the play several
times, until at last they found "some good"
in it.   At Rome I forced the play on public
favor.   A sure sign that it commanded interest was that there was always a full house.
It was not to their taste, it is true, but they
could not stay away.   For four seasons I
always selected that play for my benefit.   The
first time people blamed me; the second, they
began to be interested; the third, they were
pleased; and after that every time that I went
to Rome they asked me how soon I should
give "Othello."

HAMLET

I BECAME so much enamored of the great
English dramatist, that I was constrained to
neglect somewhat the classic school, though
I still held it in warm affection, in order to
occupy myself with a character extravagant
indeed, but nevertheless full of attraction—
that of *Hamlet.*   I chose the translations by
Giulio Carcano as the most in accord with

my taste, and for a fixed yearly payment he ceded to me "Othello" and all his other translations and abridgments from Shakspere. In the eyes of the public my form seemed too colossal for *Hamlet*. The adipose, lymphatic, and asthmatic thinker of Shakspere must change himself, according to the popular imagination, into a slender, romantic, and nervous figure; and although my *Hamlet* was judged more than flatteringly by the most authoritative critics, and by the first dramatic artist of that day, it will always take rank after my *Othello*. I do not know whether I should felicitate myself upon having incarnated that son of Mauritania; sure it is that he has done some injury to other personifications of my repertory, though not less carefully elaborated. I am bound to declare that *Hamlet, Orestes, Saul, King Lear,* and *Corrado* in "La Morte Civile," cost me no less study or application than *Othello*, and that my artistic conscience has never doubted that there was full as much merit in my interpretation of those characters as in that of the other. Nevertheless, *Othello* has always been the favorite and the best applauded; *Othello* is a sight-draft, which the public ha paid promptly every time that it has been presented.

SOPHOCLES

THE reader who has become accustomed to my small modesty will permit me to make another assertion. The part in which I have the least fault to find with myself is that of *Sofocle*, in the drama in verse of the same name by Paolo Giacometti. The play was written expressly for me; and I venture to say that the emotions of that grandiose figure are modeled so well upon my capabilities that his spoils would ill become any other artist. Yet that name, venerated as poet and as citizen, cannot boast that it ever drew a full house. Those who came were always full of enthusiasm; but though I tried it repeatedly, the audience was always scanty, and this notwithstanding that the play is one of the most meritorious that have been written in this century.

SAMSON

ANOTHER work was written expressly for me by Ippolito d'Aste — "Sansone," a bibli-

cal tragedy, rich in noble verses, striking in its
conception, and of incontestable scenic effec-
tiveness, but beyond a doubt, as a philosophi-
cal and literary production, much inferior to
"Sofocle." Yet the preëminent Greek poet
was forced, by the capriciousness and injustice of the public, to yield the primacy to the
biblical hero. This play, too, became a spe-
cialty of my repertory. I must, however,
acknowledge that my athletic figure and
powerful muscles, and the strength of my
voice, had their part in the great success of
this play. It is idle to deny that for certain
parts appropriate physical and vocal qualities
are indispensable, and are an inseparable
factor in success. It is an illusion that in the
representative arts intelligence and talent
are alone sufficient to win a great reputation. The singer may possess an admirable
method, facility in trilling, perfection in intonation; but if he has not also a fine and
powerful voice, he will never rise above mediocrity. The public demands, in addition to
talent, physical presence; in addition to art, a
sympathetic and unlabored sonority of voice.
If there is deficiency in one or another natural
gift, attention becomes dulled, enthusiasm is

not aroused, and the public sets one down in the category of the intelligent and worthy, but not in that of the eminent.

And this is not an injustice, for one is in no way constrained to join a profession of which the demands are so exacting. The public has not forced you to put yourself in a position where you must beg for its indulgence, or to expose yourself in an endeavor which is beyond your strength. Those incomplete artists are unjust who rail at the coolness of the public, at the sharpness of the critic. Such characters as *Saul, Samson,* and *Ingomar* demand an imposing form and a masculine and powerful voice, and since nature had favored me with these material advantages, I was able for long to couple my name with those of the biblical king, the hero of the Jews, and the barbarian.

IN PARIS

WHEN I had become in fair measure satisfied with my rendering of *Orosmane* in "Zaïre," of *Saul,* and of *Othello,* I persuaded my friend and associate Cesare Dondini to try our fortune at the Salle Ventadour in Paris. I carried only my art with me, and in that *mare magnum* of all earthly celebrities this proved to be a rather scant capital. In Paris, no doubt, true merit is appreciated; but if one has not the means of presenting his merit along with a pretty liberal dose of charlatanism, it is offered to deaf ears, and the few who do appreciate it are swallowed up in the indifference of the vast majority. Well, we arrived in Paris, and, thinking to flatter the national pride, we chose Voltaire's "Zaïre" for our first production. Our chief actress, Clementina Cazzola, was frightened by Ristori's great success, and declined to accompany us on this venture; all her parts were accordingly intrusted to a conscientious young actress, Alfonsina Aliprandi, who filled them with credit. *Orosmane* was acclaimed, *Zaïre* applauded, *Lusignan* (Lorenzo Piccinini) praised; but the play had lived its time, the classic type was in decadence, and our choice of a piece was criticized. We promptly produced "Saul." This sublime composition was pronounced by the Gallic critics heavy, dry, arid, incomprehensible. May Heaven pardon them! They were incapable of un-

7

derstanding it. I convinced myself that this
was really the case when I went to look for
a French translation of "Saul," in order to
have librettos prepared to promote appreciation of it, and found that fine opening, "Bell'
alba è questa," rendered, "Oh, quelle belle
matinée!" I became even more convinced
when Alexandre Dumas, *père*, maintained
that Alfieri should have made his *Saul* a
young man, and not an old one. If an acute,
many-sided, imaginative talent like that was
capable of making so nonsensical an exhibi-
tion of itself, it can easily be imagined what
the smaller fry said. Thus "Saul" shared the
fate of "Zaïre." There was applause, and
there were flattering notices, but the play
would not draw. As our last anchor of
safety, we tried "Othello." Shakspere was
the fashion, and even I became the fashion,
too! Paris was moved; and according to
her wont, being moved, she went into a state
of exultation. The Anglo-Saxon sojourners
came, too; the journalists were forced (I say
forced, because they did it greatly against
their wish) to fall into line with the general
appreciation, to float with the current, and to
bring themselves to do me justice. "Othello"

paid the expenses of our season. The most generous praises were lavished on the artists; in especial a demonstration was made by the Comédie Française, which decided, in order to do honor to the Italian actor, that on the night of his benefit several of its actors and actresses should take part in the representation. I must admit that if the French once begin to be agreeable, they do not stop halfway; and it was no small achievement to have interested the manager and the artists of that model playhouse.

At this time I formed the acquaintance of a lady who wields much influence among the publishing enterprises of North America, and she urged me to go to New York; she said that she was sure I should have great success there, particularly in "Othello," and promised me that I could count on her friendly interest as a guaranty of a favorable outcome. I hesitated, however, because of the length of the journey, of my usual diffidence as to my own ability, and, above all, of the exiguity of my finances. What means had I to fall back on in the event of a disaster? I thanked the amiable lady, and dismissed the thought.

A thousand testimonials of esteem and sympathy followed, which it would be tedious to set forth here. Through these, as by an electric flash, knowledge of our success was disseminated in Italy, and offers of new and advantageous engagements pelted Dondini like hail. In his function as manager he accepted one of these for Sicily, comprising the three chief cities of the island; and the results of that year were highly profitable for our association. So it is that with increase of fame comes increase of funds also!

Upon our return to Italy, Signora Cazzola resumed her post in the company.

We next went to Sicily, opening at Catania. The four years that I passed with Cesare Dondini were the most advantageous of my career to my artistic reputation. The public, and more than the public, my colleagues, conceded to me the palm in the rendering of several parts. They affirmed that I had no rival as *Orestes*, as *Orosmane*, as *Saul*, in the "Morte Civile," in the "Suonatrice d'Arpa," as *Sansone*, in "Pamela," and finally as *Othello*. This judgment, though of much weight, did not quench entirely my ardent desire to make myself a specialist in still other plays. At the end of my service with the Dondini company, I was engaged as chief actor for the Compagnia Reale de' Fiorentini of Naples from the first day of Lent in the year 1860. I found but small change in the atmosphere of the theater after my fifteen years of absence. Almost all those who had been attached to it in 1845 were still there. The celebrated character-actor Luigi Taddei, who had joined the company ten years before, had become old and rather infirm, and, though always admirable, appeared but seldom. Only Fanny Sadowsky, though advanced in age, retained the spirit and energy of the fair days of her triumphs. In fine, the walls of the establishment had received a coat of whitewash, but the foundations were the same. The quality of the public, too, was unchanged in that hundred-year-old theater. There were still those families who subscribed for their seats by the year, and who inserted in their marriage-contracts, as one of the conditions, a box at the Fiorentini for the bride. It was once their cherished pleasure to create or destroy the reputation of those who came before their supreme tribunal.

7*

At that time the company, subsidized by
the Bourbon government, still enjoyed the
privilege of playing in that theater without
competition, whence arose a Chinese wall
bétween the actors of that company and all
others of the peninsula; so that if any of
them happened to leave Naples for Florence,
for instance, they would ask him whether he
was going to Italy! Nevertheless, the report
of my success had broken through the pro-
tecting wall, and curiosity was at a high pitch.
Prepiani and Monti were dead, and Adamo
Alberti alone remained as director of the enterprise; and as I could remain only one year
at Naples, he had already secured my successor. Upon my arrival in Naples, Alberti
asked me, in accordance with the terms of
my contract, which gave me the right of
choice, with what play I wished to begin,
and I indicated "Zaïre." But they had no
scenery for "Zaïre," and it would hardly do
to be content with a makeshift. "All right,"
said· I; "we will take the 'Suonatrice
d'Arpa.'" But in that play Signora Sadowsky had not yet mastered her part. "Very
well; then I will give 'Oreste.'" But Bozzo,
who was cast for *Pilade*, happened just then

to be ill. "Excellent," said I; "in that case I'll play whatever you like." I divined very clearly the motive for this spirit of opposition. The good man had engaged for the next three years an actor by the name of Achille Majeroni, and he was afraid that too marked a success on my part might be hurtful to his speculation with my successor. Finally he proposed to me to open with Goldoni's "Pamela"; but the *Pamela* could not be Fanny Sadowsky. "How's that?" said I; "do you want a tragedian to begin his season with a comedy, and without the support of the leading lady at that? Well, let us have it so!" He was delighted with my answer, which certainly he had not expected, and made haste to announce my first appearance in "Pamela," as happy as if he had won in three numbers at the lottery. Many were surprised at this choice of a play, and to the many who remonstrated with me I made answer that I would not set out with grumbling at my manager; that in order to get first to the goal in a long race it was better to begin to run slowly, rather than to start off at the highest speed, with the risk of finishing second.

On the appointed evening the size and quality of our house were imposing. The court
and the first literary and artistic notabilities
were there. The friends of the old actors
had their guns cocked and primed; the journalists and pseudo-authors with whom Naples abounds were all under arms, and more
disposed to find fault than to praise. I had
before me the double task of routing the old
fogies of 1845, and of being equal to the
exaggerated renown that had preceded me;
in short, I had serious difficulties to overcome, and at the same time I had against me
the inveterate bad taste of that public, which
is not offended by a conventional cadence in
phrasing, by monotony of delivery, and by
gestures and motions worthy of Punchinello.
I was not in the least nervous in face of this
serious and really difficult undertaking. My
pulse did not count one beat more than the
normal. I neither looked at the house, nor
even saw it by chance; I identified myself
entirely with the personage whose part I was
playing (*Lord Bonfield*), and I made such an
impression on that rather hostile audience,
that at the end of every act it showed me,
first favor, then admiration, and finally enthu-

siasm. When I came to the scene in which
Pamela's father, who is thought to be a vil-
lager, reveals his true rank to *Lord Bonfield*,
and tells him his story, declaring himself to be
a count and proving it by authenticated docu-
ments, whence it results that his daughter
Pamela is worthy to become the consort of
the aristocratic and impassioned *Lord Bonfield*, I succeeded by the mobility of my
countenance, and by the feverish motions of
my body, in following every part of the tale
with such intent interest and such truth, that
without uttering a syllable I drew from the
audience a prolonged cry of enthusiasm, and
no more doubt attended the completeness of
my success. Poor Alberti! He was constrained to follow the current, and to take
steps at once to put on the stage those very
plays which he had found such excellent
reasons for not giving, and these confirmed
me emphatically in public favor. "Zaïre,"
"Oreste," "Hamlet," "Saul" transported Naples with enthusiasm.

It would be impossible to note all the
marks of esteem and appreciation which the
Neapolitans lavished upon me. Everybody
wanted to know me; everybody wished for

my friendship; everybody made it his boast
to be seen in my company on the prome-
nades and at the places of resort; and everybody would say in passing, "Here is that
most excellent fellow, our Salvine!" I had
really come to belong to them, I was no
longer my own master; and to such a point
that the burden of entertainments, visits, in-
vitations became almost oppressive. I had
secured my revenge! I had won over a public that had been confirmed in its habits; I
had convinced critics disposed to be severe,
and overcome the hostility of the envious on
the stage; and I had put the laugh on a dis-
obliging manager.

During my stay in Naples, heroic acts of
almost incredible valor were done in Sicily by
the thousand followers of Giuseppe Garibaldi, who overran the entire kingdom of the
Two Sicilies. Naples was freed from the
tyranny of the Bourbons, and received in security every free citizen of Italy. Gustavo
Modena, who had always been interdicted
from setting foot on the soil of Naples, took a
fancy to visit the Parthenopean city, and at
the same time to make himself known profes-
sionally to the Neapolitans. I encouraged

him in this project, eager again to come into relations with my old master, and to see him play; but he kept answering my letters with new doubts and difficulties. At last, however, the way seemed clear, and I busied myself with hiring the Teatro del Fondo, and with engaging several actors of other companies, who had taken advantage of the annulling of the monopoly of the Fiorentini to come to Naples. In a word, I organized a company from what I could find, but it was sufficient for Modena's purpose; and despite Alberti's unremitting hostility, I secured permission to give him my own support for a night. Modena arrived in due time at Naples, but he kept putting off the announcement of his appearance. I was able to see him only in the daytime, for I had to play every night; and every day I saw more clearly, to my deep regret, that his physical strength was failing. Finally he declared that his health would not permit him to face the judgment of the public, and that he found himself compelled to return at once to his home in Turin. It was a bitter disappointment, and a real grief to all who loved our art. I was eager to have him dine with me,

with the Signora Giulia, before his departure;
and they accepted upon condition that there
should be only the three of us. I promised,
and two days afterward they came. As can
easily be imagined, the stage formed the sta-
ple of our conversation; and I begged him,
before he left, to drop in some evening at the
Fiorentini, so that I might have his opinions
and advice upon what progress I might have
made. "I have seen you," he answered.
"How?" said I. "Where? When?" And
he replied, "I have seen you in 'Hamlet' and
in 'Saul.'" I felt as if a bucket of cold water
had been doused over my head, and for five
full minutes the conversation lapsed. He had
come twice to the Teatro de' Fiorentini without my knowing anything of it. Finally I
took courage, and asked him his opinion.
"Here it is," he answered. "Nobody can
play *Hamlet* but you; in 'Saul' my fourth
act is better than yours, but your fifth act is
better than mine." Not a word more did he
say. Ought I to appeal from this judgment,
or to be so modest as not to deem it just and
impartial? I do not think so; I should be
wanting in respect to the infallible criticism
of that unequaled judge, and should, more-

over, be false to my own conscience. Yes;
Modena's words were true, and I will tell
why, since he did not see fit to explain them.
As a fervent republican and a very bitter foe
of clericalism, into the diatribes of the fourth
act, the reproaches heaped by *Saul* on the
high priest *Ahimelech*, he put all his energy
and the conviction due to his political creed,
and he obtained extraordinary results. This
effort left him, however, prostrated with fatigue, so that he was not in a condition to
supply the great exertion demanded by the
fifth act. In my own case, since I was not
under obligation to fill before the audience
the double character of artist and of anticleri-
cal, I husbanded my strength, so that, without
weakening the fourth act, I was still in condition to give full effect to the passion, the
delirium, and the calamitous ending of that
ill-starred king.

DEATH OF MODENA

In 1861 I visited Turin as first actor and
manager of a company bearing my name.
Hardly had I arrived in the city when the sad

news came to me that Modena, my master, my
second father, had ceased to live.   I hurried
to his house to render the last tribute of my
affection.   I had the honorable though mourn-
ful office of bearing on my shoulder, with three
other faithful friends, the body of this distinguished man.   That evening, as a slight tribute
of grief, I had the theater closed, and I headed
a subscription to a fund for the erection of a
monument on the grave of the great patriot
and artist, and all the members of my company
contributed, of their own motion, a day's salary; in addition I gave a performance the proceeds of which were applied to the fund.   It
all footed up to a handsome sum, which was
placed in the hands of a committee formed of
the political friends of the dead man ; and in
addition to my collections this committee received many other liberal subscriptions from
all the provinces of Italy.

Four years passed, and having occasion to
write to Modena's widow to secure a manu-
script of "Mahomet II." which belonged to my
master, I asked her for news of the fund.
Her answer ended as follows: "Never ask me
again what has become of the money for the
monument of my Gustavo; it is a sad and dis-

graceful story." And it is a disgrace to Italy
that not yet has just honor been paid to the
memory of that inimitable artist and distinguished patriot.

To return to the chronicle of my artistic
career, in 1861 and 1862 my company was
formed of chosen artists, such as Clementina
Cazzola, Isolina Piamonti, my brother Alessandro Salvini, Guglielmo Privato, Gaetano
Voller, Gaetano Coltellini, and Luigi Biagi.
All my thought and activity were devoted to
the direction of my artists, to train them to
work together, to inspire them, so to speak, in
such manner that our productions should be
distinguished for the homogeneity, the precision, and the harmony of the rendering. I gave
all my energy to the object of surpassing the
various companies of highest rank which had
deservedly acquired a stable renown; and without fear of contradiction I can say that in this
I had satisfactory success, as was made plain
by the size and contentment of our audiences.

FRIENDLY RIVALRIES IN NAPLES

In 1863 I filled a few short engagements
with a company under the management of

Antonio Stacchini, an excellent *genre* artist,
and in the intervals of idleness I went for the
first time to London to look over the ground,
which seemed to me capable of giving a good
harvest. I visited several theaters; but the
only one which seemed to me at that time
promising for an experiment with Italian
drama was the St. James. But the demands
of the agent of that house alarmed me. After
having hunted through every corner of that
vast city, I returned to Italy, disappointed as
to my plans, but not discouraged. I happened to be at Leghorn for the sea-bathing
when the leading actor Adamo Alberti, then
manager of the Florentine Company in Naples, came there with the purpose of engaging
me with Clementina Cazzola for his theater
for three years.

Achille Majeroni, with Fanny Sadowsky
and Luigi Taddei, left the Teatro de' Fiorentini to join the Teatro del Fondo, taking with
them many of the patrician families who had
been subscribers at the Fiorentini. The sub-
scription-list at the Fondo reached the total
of 130,000 lire, while ours was only 80,000.
We had, however, great advantages over them
in the novelty of our chief actress, Clementina

RACHEL AS "PHEDRE."

Cazzola, and in our repertory of forty plays, which had never been given in Naples, and in which that admirable actress and I supported each other. Majeroni, taking advantage of the abolition of the censorship, began to offer to the public all the plays which had been placed on the index by the Bourbon government; these were not liked by the aristocratic society people, and they declared that they did not want any more of them. At the Fiorentini, on the contrary, all the new pieces were greeted with sympathy; and although our subscribers were few, the paying public crowded our house more every night. Our plays were free from all licentiousness and demagogism; they were chosen for their sentiment and literary worth, and the most fastidious audience could sit through them and experience nothing but interest and pleasure. In Lent of 1865 the tables had been turned. The Fondo theater had 60,000 lire of subscriptions on its books, and we had 140,000. Not that the artists of their company were not excellent. Achille Majeroni was an actor of splendid physical and vocal gifts, and many of his rôles were played with rare ability; but he had the fault of being

8

slightly monotonous in his cadences, and had
a systematic evenness of intonation at the
close of his periods which was unpleasant to
the ear.   Fanny Sadowsky maintained her
high promise, and with her beauty and intelligence raised for herself a firm pedestal, upon
which she stood like a statue of Canova,
adorned with grace and feeling; but even
she was affected by the same shortcomings
as her colleague Majeroni.   Luigi Taddei, a
very celebrated comedian, in many ways recalled the talent of the great Luigi Vestri;
but unfortunately he was compelled by a
stroke of paralysis to leave the stage.   To al-
leviate somewhat his unhappy financial condition, the artists of the Fondo and the Fiorentini joined forces, and gave a benefit to the
excellent and unfortunate artist.   The play
was "Oreste," and it was given at the Teatro
San Carlo with a result at once honorable
and lucrative.   Our two rival companies kept
up a constant exchange of courtesies; there
was between us an emulation in civility and
friendliness, and if there was rivalry, it was a
rivalry without bitterness, or rancor, or self-
assertion.   Finally the Fondo Company had
to abandon the contest, and at the opening

of the third year it left Naples for upper Italy. We were left undisputed masters of the field, and the Teatro de' Fiorentini was no longer able to hold the people who wanted to get in. At this time I gave Giacometti's "Morte Civile," and a little note sent to me by the celebrated author shall narrate for me what was my success. Here it is:

GAZZUOLO, December 3, 1864.

MY DEAR TOMMASO: Permit me affectionately to press your hand to thank you for the rehabilitation given to my "Morte Civile" by the power of your talent, at the Teatro de' Fiorentini, in face of the unfortunate outcome of the attempt a few evenings before at the Teatro del Fondo. If this may perhaps be counted as one among so many noble satisfactions which Art has honored herself by according to you, it is not less one for me also, with this difference, that I remain in it a debtor to your genius!

PAOLO GIACOMETTI.

We must make allowance for the joy of an author who has been applauded; it is nevertheless true that the "Morte Civile" was during the three years of my stay in Naples a necessary and safe complement to the repertory for every week.

HIS "OTHELLO" AT ITS BEST

BEFORE giving "Othello" it was my wish
to familiarize the Neapolitan public with a
class of works foreign to that which had previously been seen on the boards of that theater.
I had already played Voltaire's "Zaïre" several
times, and other plays characterized by vehemence of passion, and it seemed to me that
the time had come to try the effect of the
implacable *Moor of Venice* upon my audience.   It is very seldom that I have attained
satisfaction with myself in that rôle; I may
say that in the thousands of times that I have
played it I can count on the fingers of one
hand those when I have said to myself, "I
can do no better," and one of those times was
when I gave it at the Teatro de' Fiorentini.
It seemed that evening as if an electric current connected the artist with the public.
Every sensation of mine was transfused into
the audience; it responded instantaneously to
my sentiment, and manifested its perception
of my meanings by a low murmuring, by a
sustained tremor.   There was no occasion for
reflection, nor did the people seek to discuss

me; all were at once in unison and concord.
Actor, *Moor*, and audience felt the same impulse, were moved as one soul. I cannot describe the cries of enthusiasm which issued
from the throats of those thousands of persons
in exaltation, or the delirious demonstrations
which accompanied those scenes of love, jealousy, and fury; and when the shocking catastrophe came, when the *Moor*, recognizing that
he has been deceived, cuts short his days, so
as not to survive the anguish of having slain
the guiltless *Desdemona*, a chill ran through
every vein, and, as if the audience had been
stricken dumb, ten seconds went by in absolute silence. Then came a tempest of cries
and plaudits, and countless summonses before
the curtain. When the demonstration was
ended, the audience passed out amid an in-
distinct murmur of voices, and collected in
groups of five, eight, or twelve everywhere
in the neighborhood of the theater; then, re-
uniting as if by magnetic force, they came back
into the theater, demanded the relighting of
the footlights, and insisted that I should come
on the stage again, though I was half un-
dressed, to receive a new ovation. This
unparalleled and spontaneous demonstration

8*

is among the most cherished memories of my career, for it ranks among such as an artist rarely obtains.

A SCENE AT THE DANTE CENTENARY

IN 1865 a celebration of the sixth centenary of the divine poet was organized in Florence, and the municipality invited me, with Adelaide Ristori, Ernesto Rossi, and Gaetano Gattinelli, to illustrate some tableaux-vivants by reciting the original lines of Dante. The choice was left to me, and I selected the first and the thirty-third cantos of the "Inferno"; I was asked besides to recite a part of the ninth canto of the "Purgatorio," the description of the Gate of Paradise. At that time I was president of a society of mutual succor for Italian dramatic artists, which I had myself founded in Naples, and which was in a very prosperous state. I took with me to Florence the banner of my society, that it might figure among those of other associations of Italy. In the procession there were united with me as representatives of the dramatic art, besides the artists I have named, more than a hundred others,

among them many comedians. Our beautiful
banner, designed by the celebrated painter
Morelli, as well as the reunion of so many representatives of our art, made a pleasing impression on the public, which had assembled
from all Italy, and our passage in the procession
was especially distinguished by loud applause.
On the evening of the tableaux Ristori, Rossi,
and Gattinelli were admirable. The Teatro
Pagliano presented a truly imposing spectacle.
King Victor Emmanuel, the senate, the am-
bassadors, the ministers, the army, the courts,
the arts, industry, commerce — in a word, every
caste of society was represented, and that great
house was too small to hold the immense crowd
which packed itself uselessly about the doors
of the theater in the vain hope of enjoying the
spectacle. As the reciter of the first canto, I
was naturally the first to present myself on
the stage. My entrance was greeted with
sympathetic applause. When I reached the
point where the divine poet symbolizes in the
wolf the Roman Curia, and says:

> Molti son gli animali a cui s'ammoglia
> E più saranno ancora, finchè l'veltro
> Verrà, che la farà morir di doglia![1]

[1] Many are the animals with which she wives, and there shall be
more yet, till the hound shall come that will make her die of grief.—
C. E. NORTON.

I looked fixedly at the king, and stood for
several seconds without speaking. The audience caught the allusion on the instant, and a
storm of applause burst out as if it would
never stop. I believe that Victor Emmanuel
at that moment would have preferred to be at
the hunt rather than in the theater. The people persisted in their applause, and in crying:
"Viva il Re! Viva l'Italia!" His Majesty
did not understand, or did not wish to understand, the allusion which had aroused this
enthusiasm, and hesitated for a time, but at
last he was compelled to rise, and with appearance of great excitement thanked the people
several times. The applause was so tremendous that I thought the theater would fall
about my ears.

A MEMORABLE PERFORMANCE WITH RISTORI

To my pleasure in having given occasion to
that political demonstration was added another
on the two nights of that same occasion when
the tragedy of "Francesca da Rimini" was
given at the Teatro Niccolini before houses of
equal quality.to that of the Dante recitations
at the Pagliano. Adelaide Ristori was *Fran-*

cesca, Ernesto Rossi was *Paolo*, Lorenzo Piccinini was *Guido da Polenta*, Antonio Bozzo was the *Page*, and I filled the part of *Lanciotto*. Adelaide Ristori did not fall behind her worldwide fame; Ernesto Rossi surpassed himself, and that is not saying little; Lorenzo Piccinini was acclaimed; and they say that my success was a revelation. The betrayed husband of *Francesca* had had until then interpreters who had not brought out the loftiness of that generous, loyal, and loving nature; he had generally been conceived as a stern, tyrannical, and vindictive husband, and the character had been played by artists accustomed to depict the most revolting characters. I made him an affectionate husband, worthy of pity in his misfortune, and torn by anguish in the just recriminations which he hurls at the guilty pair, and the public felt sympathy with the afflicted husband and betrayed prince, and disapproval, blame, and condemnation for his betrayers. It seemed to me that I had penetrated to the moral of the tragedy. It was not for nothing that Dante placed adulterers in the circle of the tormented. The new interpretation of this part spread very quickly among cultivators of the Italian stage, and I received warm felicitations even from persons

who were not known to me. At the end of
the third act Adelaide Ristori gave me a kiss
of admiration. At the end of the fourth the
public, which by etiquette had been constrained
to silence, called my companions and me many
times before the curtain, and when the tragedy
was completed it seemed as though the ovation
would never stop, and we were obliged to repeat
the play on the following night to content
those who had not been able to obtain tickets
for the first night. A marble slab in the vesti-
bule of the pit commemorates in letters of gold
this eventful performance.

After a few days I returned to Naples, and
when I appeared again on the stage my return was applauded as a son is greeted when
he comes back to his family—a most unusual
thing in the theaters of Naples. The government had named me by decree a Knight of
St. Maurice and St. Lazarus, and the artists of
the Fiorentini Company united in a subscription to present me with the cross, bearing the
following inscription on the back:

To Tommaso Salvini,
Prince of the Stage,
His Companions in Art.

You can imagine how pleased I was with this amiable proof of esteem and affection offered to me by my brothers in art.

AN AMENDE FROM PRINCE HUMBERT

In 1863, while I was with the manager Antonio Stacchino, we had occasion to play a few times at the Teatro Carcano in Milan. One evening Humbert of Savoy, the son of Victor Emmanuel, who was sojourning at Monza, came and stayed through the whole play. As I was on the point of going on the stage for the fourth act, an aide-de-camp of the prince, who is now a general, handed me a package, and said, " In the name of His Royal Highness." I thanked him hastily, put the package in my pocket, and went on to proceed with the act. When I came off I hurried to my dressing-room and undid the packet, expecting to find some souvenir ; but it was money—ten napoleons in gold. I confess that at sight of it my pride was wounded. What was I to do? I did not care to refuse the gift, as I had done some time before with the Prince of Carignan, for

fear of offending the son of our great king;
therefore I decided to keep the money, hoping
that the future would give me an opportunity
to clear myself of the suspicion of being a
venal artist. In 1865 and 1866 I had the
pleasure of enjoying the acquaintance of the
estimable wife of Senator Vigliani, who was
then prefect at Naples, an Englishwoman,
highly educated, and an impassioned admirer
of Shakspere. In the course of my visits I
took occasion to refer to what had happened
at Milan, and to express my sense of injury.
The high-spirited lady was surprised, and
seemed even to show real regret, and I could
not doubt that she would speak of it to some
frequenter of the Prince's court. One day
when I was on the terrace of the prefecture
with many gentlemen and ladies who had
been invited to watch the passages of the
masks, for it was carnival time, the same officer who had placed the packet in my hands in
Milan, and with whom I was on the footing
of acquaintanceship, came to my side and
said, "Salvini, when do you take your benefit?" "Some night before long," I answered.
"Let me know when the time comes," said
he; "for His Royal Highness desires to be

present." I announced "Francesca da Rimini" for my benefit, and the Prince, punctually, as is the habit in the House of Savoy, came to the theater. On the morrow I received the following letter:

MOST ESTEEMED SIR: His Royal Highness was greatly interested by the performance which took place yesterday evening, 16th instant, at the Teatro de' Fiorentini, and in which you gave new evidence of your powerful dramatic genius. The august Prince is full of admiration for an artist who has had the ability to raise himself to your well-merited fame, and, desiring to give you a sincere attestation of his particular esteem, he has taken satisfaction in intrusting to me the pleasant charge of presenting to you, in his august name, the pin in brilliants which I transmit to you with this note. It is a pleasure to me to be the interpreter of the kind feelings of His Royal Highness toward you; and I take advantage of the opportunity to assure you of my own very high consideration. The Major-General, 1st aide-de-camp. REVEL.

I opened the inclosure, and discovered on the pin beneath the royal crown the letters "U. S.," for Umberto Savoja. The Prince had had the delicacy to compensate me with usury for a mistake, very probably not his own; and I could do no less than exclaim in my heart: "Viva Umberto! Viva l'Arte!"

At this time it was my misfortune to see my
illustrious and beloved colleague Clementina
Cazzola waste away from day to day in the
clutches of an incurable disease. The doctors
pronounced that if the good creature persisted
in the exercise of her art she would shorten
her life, and she was constrained to retire
from the stage in the hope that rest and quiet
would conjure away the menace to her health.
In her absence the whole weight of artistic
responsibility at the Teatro de' Fiorentini fell
upon me, and I put forth every effort of which
I was capable to make the loss to the management as light as possible. I was obliged
to feign satisfaction while my heart was full
of pain, and this throughout two years. I
sought to quench my trials in my art, and
while I was struggling between laughter and
tears, art found profit in the combination of
emotions due to my afflicted state. In that
year, 1866, Paolo Giacometti delivered to me
the tragedy of "Sofocle," which I had suggested to him, and in studying that sublime
character I perceived that with the death of
the protagonist I could identify my own af-
flicting position. *Sofocle* dies at the moment
when the crown of olive decreed by the

Greek senate is brought to him, and when
his sons return from the field to announce
to him that the haughty *Alcibiade*, out
of respect for the grand tragic poet, re-
nounces his intended destruction of the
necropolis where repose his ancestors; thus
Sofocle is happy with the assurance of
resting with his own. He dies surrounded
by his family, honored and acclaimed by
his fellow-citizens, while his nephew with
his lyre chants in his stead the pæan, the
sacred hymn to the fatherland. He dies
following the strains of that melody, un-
consciously moving his fingers, and fancying
that it is he who is singing the hymn of
Athens to his lyre; he dies with a smile on
his lips, with joy in his heart—but he dies! I,
too, smiled, but in place of joy I had death
in my heart. I, too, sang the hosanna, but
the "De Profundis" held my soul. I, too,
was filled with joy from the love and acclaim
of my countrymen, and the relative positions of the Hellenic poet and the Italian
tragedian were so closely parallel that my
rendering of his emotions could not but be
true. A letter from the author, which I
have preserved, will tell more eloquently than

I could the effect produced by the play and
its interpretation:

MY DEAR TOMMASO: Thank you, my friend, for the
fine account which you have kindly given me of the outcome of my "Sofocle"; thank you for the papers you
have sent me, from which I should have formed an idea,
if your letter had not been enough, of the reception given
to my piece, as well as of your sublimity in acting it. I
have not seen you, and who can tell when I shall see you,
in the guise of the Homer of tragedy, and I am extremely
sorry for it; for if I had been present at the play I should
have enjoyed one of those moments which are perhaps the
only happy ones in an author's life, and I should have im-
printed a fraternal kiss upon your forehead, which is glo-
rified by the flame of genius. When an author offers his
creation to an artist, and this artist who is to bring it before
the world of letters receives it with a religious respect,
meditates on it, and magnifies it, he acquires a sacred claim
to the esteem and affection of the poet. To your worthy
colleagues who, so far as I have seen by the accounts,
have seconded you admirably well, I beg that you will
give assurance of my gratitude. You did well to suppress
a few verses which might have proved a clog upon the
action or an obstacle to your conception; and as to your
idea of having a string of the lyre snap as *Sofocle* dies,
there could be nothing either more opportune or more
poetic: I compliment you upon it. I send you a kiss;
and receive from my wife, with her most distinguished
service, her grateful appreciation of the success of "Sofocle." Yours always,

PAOLO GIACOMETTI.

GAZZUOLO, April 10, 1866.

Nothing worthy of telling happened to me in 1867. At the head of a company of artists of medium ability I traveled through the Italian cities, finding everywhere the sympathy of the public; this was satisfying to my pride, but the alarming condition of my excellent colleague overwhelmed the triumphs of the artist. In 1868 I continued in the management of my company, with Virginia Marini as first actress, who in 1864, 1865, and 1866 had been with us at Naples, under my direction and the counsels of Clementina Cazzola. She had an iron will, unwearying application to study, surprising native talent, with a sympathetic and harmonious voice, which caused to be overlooked her defect of unconscious imitation.

SALVINI AND VICTOR EMMANUEL

In the summer of 1868 I was at the Politeama Theater in Florence with Virginia Marini. Florence was then the provisional capital of the kingdom, and from King Victor Emmanuel down all the notabilities of Italy had a standing appointment to meet in the

evening at the Politeama. The king seemed
to take much interest in my playing, for he
did not stay away a single night. I have been
asked which rôles seemed to appeal most to
him; they were *Ingomar* in the "Figlio delle
Selve," *Sansone* in the tragedy of the same
name, and *Van Bruch* in "Giosuè il Guardacoste"—three strong, ardent, robust, loyal
characters. It seemed as if he mirrored himself in them; and when I passed near the
royal box after having saluted the public,
I would hear the voice of a stentor shout,
"Bravo! Bravo!" It was the king.

One evening, perhaps more pleased than
usual, he took from his finger a diamond ring,
and commissioned the Marchese di Brem to
bring it to me on the stage. The marquis
said to me: "His Majesty begs you to accept
this reminder of his royal admiration. You
must prize it, for he has worn it for five years."
A few days after this, at nine o'clock one morning, my servant came to my bedroom and told
me that there was a gentleman in the draw-
ing-room who desired to speak to me at once.
I was a little vexed, and I said: "How? At
this time of the morning? But I am still in
bed." Then I heard a voice calling from the

next room: "Excuse me, Salvini; I am the
Marchese di Brem, and I come from the king
to say to you that His Majesty wishes to see
you at once at the Pitti. Dress yourself as
fast as you can, and I will wait at your door
with the carriage." So I put on my dress-
coat and went to the palace. The marquis
accompanied me to the royal antechamber,
where I found many people awaiting audience, and, informing me that the officer on
duty would call my name, he left me with the
words, "I warn you that His Majesty takes
you for a republican."

Among those who were waiting there were
many diplomatists, officers of rank, the Genoese sculptor Varni, whom I knew, and a
pretty young girl who did not mingle with the
others, and whom I expected would be summoned first before the king. Soon two gen-
erals, whose names I forget, came out of the
royal apartments, and I heard my name spoken
by the officer at the door. I advanced to the
door of the first room, after which there were
five others to traverse before reaching His
Majesty; and I saw at the end of the vista, as
in a picture framed by the five doors, the form
of Victor Emmanuel, who awaited my ap-

proach with legs and feet joined, and his hands
in the pockets of his wide trousers.   When I
reached the threshold of the last door, I halted,
and in the position and with the military salute
of a veteran, I said, "Your Majesty!"   The
king advanced toward me, and, extending his
hand cordially, said:

"My dear Salvini, I am very glad to see
you and to know you personally."

"Your Majesty," said I, "I am greatly
flattered by the honor which Your Majesty
does me."

"My dear Salvini," said His Majesty, "a
man of *your* merit flatters other people by
his acquaintance."   He took two cigars and
offered one to me.   "Do you smoke?"

"Yes, Your Majesty.   But I am an old
corporal, and smoke only Tuscan cigars."

"Light this one, and tell me what you
think of it."   He lighted a match and handed
it to me to light a great Havana cigar; then
he lighted his own, and approached a window looking out on the Boboli Gardens.   "I
wanted to tell you how much I admire you
as an artist.   You are a republican, are you
not?"

"Yes, Your Majesty.   But when there are

kings who are loyal, warlike, and honorable, like you, it is possible to be a constitution-alist."

"Thanks; thanks. It is very true that I live only for my nation. The battle-field is the post of my predilection. Politics cut the grass under my feet; and sometimes, just as you say in the 'Figlio delle Selve,' 'I could rend the world,' I could rend the walls of my room. And I do not think that you have been a flatterer in calling me 'Re Galan-tuomo.' It seems to me that I am in truth that; but I could equally be a loyal pres-ident of your republic if I were not under the obligation of preserving a crown which has been transmitted to me, and which dates from centuries."

"Your Majesty, no one contests that obli-gation; but even if it were a burden for you, with your loyalty you would sustain it easily."

"Thanks; thanks. For that matter, loyalty is traditional in the House of Savoy; it is in the blood, and I have no merit in observing it and in causing it to be maintained."

Up to this point all the words of the dia-logue, spoken as we were both leaning on the front of the window, remain as if in-

9*

scribed in my memory, and I can be sure of
their exactitude. I made several attempts to
draw the conversation upon the needs of art,
the necessity of providing for its restoration;
but when I sought to express my views, the
king answered that the theater could not
deteriorate since it had representatives like
me, that my name was an honor to the
country, that artists must spring up from my
example; in fine, with these praises he closed
my mouth, and went back to politics. Among
very many expressions which have escaped
my mind one has remained with me, and its
intimation has come true: that he would be
content to die on the day when he had been
able to set his foot in Rome. Can you, dear
reader, tell me the motive of this frankness,
of these royal confidences, to me, a dramatic
artist? I have not yet succeeded in explaining it. Perhaps, under the impression of the
strong and generous characters that I had
been playing, he fancied that he was opening
his mind to *Sansone*, to *Ingomar*, or to *Van
Bruch;* and when, in my hints about the
needs of art, he was brought back to the
prosaic Salvini, he changed the subject to get
back to the atmosphere which gave him plea-

sure. A good hour had passed, and my cigar was nearly finished, when I permitted myself to deplore the fate of the persons who on my account were waiting in the antechamber. Victor Emmanuel answered me: "Let them wait. You are certainly more occupied than they, and I do not believe that for that you wish to go away so soon." "I will go away," I answered, "when Your Majesty gives me the command." Upon this he approached the writing-table, and taking up a packet, gave it to me, with the words: "Take this. I want you to have a souvenir of our acquaintance, and I hope that this will not be the last time that I shall have the pleasure of talking with you. I salute you." He again held out his hand to me, and I went away, saying: "I am at the orders of Your Majesty." When I had reached the second room, I heard a loud ringing, and while the officer on service was advancing to the king, Victor Emmanuel called out behind me: "I shall see you this evening," informing me thus that he would come to the Politeama. I went back to my house charmed with the affable, frank, and familiar manner of the "Re Galantuomo." I opened the parcel which he had given me, and in it was a box with the royal cipher containing the cross of Officer of the Crown of Italy. A few days afterward a very different cross was fixed in my heart, a cross of strife and of mourning — Clementina Cazzola was dead !

OFF FOR SOUTH AMERICA — A STORM

CONVINCED that, owing both to lack of public and government support, and to the growing carelessness as to details among Italian managers and actors, dramatic art was suffering a partial eclipse in Italy, after a tour in 1869 in Spain and Portugal, which, owing to the very heavy expenses, and to the revolutionary movements in progress, produced but scanty returns, I decided to accept the offer of a respected South-American impresario. I was anxious to test the question whether in the New World work and study could look for an adequate reward; and I was attracted also by the foreign appreciation of my country through the agency of art.

The new company which I formed for the year 1871 was made up in part of artists who were in Florence at the time, and in part of others whom I knew by reputation. Isolina Piamonti, a clever and sympathetic actress, with a melodious voice and an attractive face; Signor and Signora Aiudi, with their daughter Pierina, who afterward became one of the best younger leading ladies on the stage; Lorenzo Piccinini, and Domenico Giagnoni, were my chief supporters, and with them I had twenty of lesser rank whom I need not name. This was a company which for South America might be called extremely good; it was certainly one of the best that had ever played in those countries. Before setting out, I gave twelve representations in Bologna, to get the company well organized and working in unison, selecting those plays which I meant to give in America. At the close of the Lenten season, we all went to Genoa, and embarked aboard the steamer *Isabella*. The cost of the voyage both ways for the entire company was paid by our impresario, Señor Pestalardo of Buenos Ayres, with which city the South-American experience of our company was to begin. The national festival fell just at the time when we were due at Buenos Ayres, and that of Montevideo was to be celebrated during our stay there. Everything was well planned, organized, and provided for, so that the speculation could not fail; the impresario and I counted on sharing a handsome profit, almost a fortune, as a result of the tour.

It was my first voyage to America, the first time that I dared the ocean in a nutshell; and, whatever may be said, this experience must produce a certain impression upon anybody. Hardly had we entered the Gulf of Lyons, which is traditionally unkind to the sailor, when a tempest burst upon us, so furious that we carried away one of our masts, and had our sails torn to ribbons, and suffered some damage about the decks. All the passengers were compelled to keep below to avoid danger from the waves. I begged the captain's permission to remain awhile on the bridge to admire that imposing spectacle of irritated nature. To tell the truth, my desire to admire the fury of Neptune had only a secondary place in my mind. I was terrified at the idea of being drowned like a rat in my state-room berth, and I fostered the vain hope that since I was a very strong swimmer I might be able to save myself in

the event of shipwreck. So far as I could, in
the midst of the violent motion, and my alarm
at the danger, I made my observations.
What a magnificent spectacle it was! The
sky was veiled with impenetrable clouds; the
sea was a confused mass of black velvet
drapery with tufts of white lace, moved and
changed in countless ways by the violent
gusts, and hurled with a crash against the
sides of our ship. The rain beat against my
face, and the lamps shot fitful rays over the
horrible but majestic scene, while the detona-
tions of thunder, and the vivid gleams of the
lightning, recalled to my mind the siege of
Rome.

At daybreak we found ourselves running
in dangerous proximity to the African coast.
The ship's prow was turned toward Gibraltar,
and we made that port with difficulty. It required three days to put the vessel in condition to go to sea again.

A MODEL FOR OTHELLO

At Gibraltar I spent my time studying the
Moors. I was much struck by one very fine

figure, majestic in walk, and Roman in face, except for a slight projection of the lower lip. The man's color was between copper and coffee, not very dark, and he had a slender mustache, and scanty curled hair on his chin. Up to that time I had always made up *Othello* simply with my mustache, but after seeing that superb Moor I added the hair on the chin, and sought to copy his gestures, movements, and carriage.   Had I been able I should have imitated his voice also, so closely did that splendid Moor represent to me the true type of the Shaksperian hero. *Othello* must have been a son of Mauritania, if we can argue from *Iago's* words to *Roderigo:* "He goes into Mauritania"; for what else could the author have intended to imply but that the Moor was returning to his native land?

AT MONTEVIDEO

By reason of adverse winds and weather our voyage to Montevideo occupied forty-two days, and when the tender of the steamship company came to meet us, it was with the

melancholy announcement that yellow fever
had broken out in Buenos Ayres, and that the
death-rate was eight hundred a day. This
was depressing news, especially to me who
had submitted to the discomforts of so long a
voyage, and had punctually paid my artists
thirty per cent. above their regular salary,
and ten francs of extra pay each, during a
month and a half of idleness, in the hope of
replenishing my greatly diminished exchequer
with the fruits of my art. But much more
than by my personal hardships, and the expenditure of a considerable sum, I was occupied by my responsibility for the safety of my
companions, whom I had involuntarily led
into this predicament. My impresario had
taken refuge in the country beyond Buenos
Ayres, and there was no way of communi-
cating with that city, since the sanitary cor-
don fenced it in, and the telegraph was in
operation only for government service. I did
not know a soul in the country, I did not
speak the language, and for a moment I felt
bewildered. On landing, I soon found myself with Signor Sivori, a wealthy Genoese
merchant, who had been commissioned by my
impresario to place himself at my disposition

and to be my guide and helper. The excellent man asked me whether I was in need of funds, but I answered him that I was in need of nothing but a theater. Sivori told me that that had been provided for as soon as the epidemic had appeared in Buenos Ayres, and that the Solis Theater, the best in Montevideo, was at my disposal. A day later our first announcement was issued; but I am sure that the natives, when they read my name on the posters, asked themselves whether I was a tenor or a ballet-dancer. I opened with the "Morte Civile," and the next day there was no further question as to what I was. The newspapers and the Italian residents had made my quality public, and signs of general satisfaction were manifest. After the first night the theater was always crowded. It was the custom of the country to give only three representations a week, but I was requested to give four, to content those who wished to see me oftener. The house, at opera prices, could hold no more than about $3000; but for my benefit night the receipts were $4500, for everybody wanted boxes and orchestra chairs, and the best seats were at a premium. I received a great number of presents, and wreaths and bouquets enough to cover the whole stage.

In connection with this benefit at Montevideo occurred a rather curious episode. As I have said, King Victor Emmanuel had presented me with a diamond which he had habitually worn. On account of my devotion to the "Re Galantuomo," I never took this off my finger, except in those cases in which artistic considerations forbade the wearing of it. One night when the "Morte Civile" was played, I had to take the ring off, because it would not have been proper to retain it in my character of a convict fleeing from prison, and, as was my custom, I placed it with my watch and chain at the back of my dressing-table. After the play a number of people came to my room while I was dressing, to congratulate me, and my servant handed me my watch and chain, but forgot the ring. My attention was distracted by the conversation of so many people, and I did not notice the absence of the ring; but when I came to go to bed I perceived it, and sent my man to the theater to recover it. The keeper did not live in the building, and all the doors of the theater were closed. The next morning my

servant got up very early and hurried to
the theater, but the sweepers had already put
the actors' rooms in order, and my ring was
no longer to be found.   Had I lost my finger
I should not have felt more lively regret.   I
lodged a complaint with the police, and several persons were arrested; I had notices
posted promising a liberal reward; I had the
form of the diamond lithographed with a description of the ring, and sent copies to all
the jewelers of America and Europe; but I
got no word of it, and never recovered it.   All
Montevideo talked of this unfortunate accident.   On my benefit night, while I was re-
ceiving the ovations of the public, and was
almost buried in the flowers that were thrown
to me, a beautiful child of five or six years
advanced with a silver salver in his hand, and
held out to me a small object which was
upon it.   As I bent down to kiss the little
fellow, a quantity of flowers thrown from a
box struck the salver, and caused the little
packet to fall, and I lost sight of it in the
mass of flowers.   The curtain fell, and while
the audience was demanding me before the
curtain a number of people from the wings
swarmed around me to find the object which

FRANCESCO LOMBARDI.

had gone astray; but I was distrustful on account of my previous loss, and shouted in a loud voice: "Off the stage, all of you!" My imperious and threatening command caused the stage to be evacuated at once, while the little child who had brought the gift fled, terrified and weeping. I began a search alone among the flowers, and I soon found the object, which had fallen out of its box. It proved to be a very beautiful brilliant, to which was attached a card with the words:

You have lost the ring of a King;
The Republicans of Montevideo restore it to you.

The kind thought gave me great pleasure, and the ring was superb; still it could not replace that which had been stolen.

During our stay of two months at Montevideo the epidemic at Buenos Ayres ceased, and communication was reopened. Shortly afterward I announced our last appearance, with "Giosue il Guardacoste" ("Joshua the Coast-guard"). All the arrangements were made with the steamer *America* to carry the company to Buenos Ayres, whence no sanitary bulletins had been issued for two weeks.

So lively was the sympathy felt for me by all classes that on my farewell night the audience was not like the public paying homage to an artist: it was an affectionate family which saw with grief the departure of a well-loved member. In the midst of the applause and *bravi*, I distinguished the cry as if with one voice: "*Otra vez! Otra vez!*" ("Once more! Once more!"), with the sense that I should stay one night more to repeat my last play; and there was no way of stopping this cry until I had expressed my formal consent. I secured a delay of twenty-four hours from the management of the steamship company, so that I should not miss my engagement at Buenos Ayres. On the morning following this final representation, two hours before our sailing-time, as I was preparing my small private baggage, I heard a confused sound in the distance, mingled with martial strains, coming from several directions. As I arranged the objects upon my toilet-table I said to myself: "It remains to be seen whether there is some commotion which will prevent us from getting off!" In a little while two gentlemen presented themselves, one an Italian, the other a native, in dress-coats and white cravats and gloves, and requested the favor of accompanying me on board the *America*. I accepted with pleasure, but I could not make out the occasion of this request. The Italian then told me: "The citizens of Montevideo with the resident Italian colony, of whom we are the delegates, wish the honor and pleasure of accompanying you to the steamer." I then first understood that I was the object of a popular demonstration, and I answered the gentlemen that I was at their orders. I left the baggage to my servant, and descended the stairs with the two delegates, one on each side of me.

When I reached the street two bands struck up, and a great shout of "Viva Salvini!" arose from the throats of a crowd numbering thousands. The streets through which I was to pass were strewn with flowers, the windows were hung with draperies, and filled with ladies and children, who threw down flowers; as to the men, they were either in the procession, or standing at the doors of their houses, holding their hats in the air and shouting. Our advance was very slow on account of the immense crowd which packed the streets, and although I was surrounded by an escort of

gentlemen who requested the people to make
way for me, we were often compelled to stop,
our path being wholly blocked. At short intervals a pause was made, while addresses
were read to me in Spanish or Italian. When
the reading stopped, the cheers would begin
again, and in this way we at last reached the
mole, upon which had been erected during
the night a large arch of greens and flowers,
under which I had to pass. But first all the
addresses were presented to me engrossed on
parchment, and the people wanted to place
around my body an enormous wreath tied
with the colors of Italy and of Uruguay. It
was not possible for me to walk with this
rather voluminous decoration on my back,
and I passed under the triumphal arch car-
rying the wreath in my hands, with the aid
of the citizen delegates. Two tugs dressed
with flags were waiting to take me out to the
America. The bands and many citizens went
on board of one, and with the two delegates
I embarked on the other. At my side I found
old Signor Sivori, with tears in his eyes! Before proceeding to the *America* the two tugs
steamed around the harbor, passing alongside
all the men-of-war of various nations which

were stationed at Montevideo. The sailors manned the yards, and the officers were drawn up on the quarter-decks, and all cheered while their flags were dipped in salute. The *America* sounded her whistle to summon her passengers on board, and then a thunderous shout arose from the mole; it was the parting greeting of the people of Montevideo. I went aboard the *America* with my head whirling from so great a manifestation of esteem, and I found my colleagues so full of excitement and emotion that they embraced and kissed me.

BUENOS AYRES AND RIO DE JANEIRO

At Buenos Ayres I found the populace saddened by the recent epidemic (which had not left a single family unscathed), and in need of distraction and of breathing an atmosphere of less depression, and the Teatro Colon was always filled. Almost all the boxes were closed with gratings, for the families in mourning did not wish to be deprived of the pleasure of the theater, but did not care to appear openly; so it seemed as if I were playing in a convent or a harem. I heard people applauding me, but I could not see them. In success and financial returns, Buenos Ayres was not behind Montevideo; but we lost the national festivals in both cities — occasions which are always highly profitable to a theater. From Buenos Ayres I went to Rio de Janeiro, where I was disappointed in not finding the Emperor Dom Pedro, who was traveling in Europe. Nevertheless the Princess Regent, daughter of the Emperor, did not miss a single night at our theater, and on the evening of my benefit she had me summoned to her box, and presented to me a beautiful solitaire, which was handed to me by her consort, the Comte d'Eu. She honored me with an invitation to the imperial palace, and I found her of the most exquisite amiability.

I met no actor of distinction in South America. The theaters were busy with *zarzuela*, as *bouffe* operas are called in Spanish, and these they gave with much spirit and correctness. The audiences show interest, as do all those of the Latin races, but they are much quieter than in Italy. They rise easily to enthusiasm, and as easily forget their impressions.

ERNESTO ROSSI

AFTER the close of my tour in South America, I returned to Italy, having signed an agreement for the carnival-season at the Teatro Valle in Rome. I had some time to spare, so I gave first a few performances at Bologna and at Naples.

It was, I believe, at about this time that the proposition was made to me that I should play *Pylades*, in Alfieri's "Oreste," with Ernesto Rossi. I have always been delighted at an opportunity to join forces with artists of real worth, and I accepted the offer with the greatest pleasure, all the more so because the part of *Pylades*, in my opinion, has the advantage of lending itself to the production of a great effect with comparatively light fatigue. Be very sure of your lines, keep under control any exuberance in your vocal power, mark the positions liberally, accentuate your phrasing in just measure, hold the interest and curiosity of your audience by the play of your expression, be natural and simple while yet maintaining the dignity of the buskin, and the part of *Pylades* is mastered. I had be-

fore this seen Ernesto Rossi in other parts of
the highest importance, such as *Paolo* in
" Francesca da Rimini," *Romeo,* and *Hamlet.*
There was a time when, in the last of these
parts, the Italian public considered him as
superior to all others who had essayed it.
Whether this judgment was right or wrong,
it is indubitable that in that rôle he satisfied
the canons of Italian taste more perfectly
than those of the Anglo-Saxon. While he
was still young, his sympathetic face and his
voice were well adapted to Shakspere's eccentric personage, as, indeed, to all rôles in
which the passion of love was dominant. I
do not believe there ever was an artist who
could pronounce the words, " I love you ! "
as Ernesto Rossi said them. The word
"love" sounded well on his lips, but that of
"rage" seemed astonished to fall from them,
and out of place. Impassioned characters
found in him an innate comprehension, but
he could not sink himself sufficiently in such
as were virile and imposing; this was from
no defect in his ability, but owing to lack of
natural aptitude for such parts. Many of the
parts which he played, and which won renown for him, were by his fine and keen in-

tellect, and by his unwearied study, fashioned
and polished like a diamond. The cutting of
the gem was perfect, its rays projected their
multiform colors and dazzled and charmed;
yet it could not be maintained that it was of
pure water. It had a faint straw tinge, in-
distinguishable except to experts, but visible
to the experienced, to the intelligent, and to
careful analysts, and this almost impercepti-
ble tinge was the fact that the art did not
sufficiently conceal the man. Very frequently
the man himself would be betrayed in a gesture, or an expression, or in the voice. While
the audience was impressed by the actor's innumerable endowments, and had before its
eyes the very personage and passion that he
was portraying, of a sudden its illusion would
vanish, and it would be reminded of the man
who was playing a part, who was studying
his inflections, and designing his motions.
In Ernesto Rossi this small defect is like a
mole on the face of a beautiful woman, which
may even be looked upon as a charm.

FIRST TRIP TO THE UNITED STATES

AFTER a few months of rest, I resolved to
get together a new company, selecting those
actors and actresses who were best suited
to my repertory. The excellent Isolina
Piamonti was my leading lady; and my brother Alessandro, an experienced, conscientious, and versatile artist, supported me. An
Italian theatrical speculator proposed to me
a tour in North America, to include the chief
cities of the United States; and although I
hesitated not a little on account of the ignorance of the Italian language prevailing in
that country, I accepted, influenced somewhat
by my desire to visit a region which was
wholly unknown to me. Previous to cross-
ing the ocean I had several months before
me, and these served me to get my company
in training.

My first impressions of New York were
most favorable. Whether it was the benefit
of a more vivifying atmosphere, or the comfort of the national life, or whether it was
admiration for that busy, industrious, work-
loving people, or the thousands of beautiful

women whom I saw in the streets, free and proud in carriage, and healthy and lively in aspect, or whether it was the thought that these citizens were the great-grandchildren of those high-souled men who had known how to win with their blood the independence of their country, I felt as if I had been born again to a new existence. My lungs swelled more freely as I breathed the air impregnated with so much vigor and movement, and so much liberty, and I could fancy that I had come back to my life of a youth of twenty, and was treading the streets of republican Rome. With a long breath of satisfaction I said to myself: "Ah, here is life!" Within a few days my energy was redoubled. A lively desire of movement, not a usual thing with me, had taken possession of me in spite of myself. Without asking myself why, I kept going here and there, up and down, to see everything, to gain information; and when I returned to my rooms in the evening, I could have set out again to walk still more. This taught me why Americans are so un-wearied and full of business. Unfortunately I have never mastered English sufficiently to converse in that tongue; had I possessed that privilege, perhaps my stay in North America would not have been so short, and perhaps I might have figured on the English stage. What an enjoyment it would have been to me to play Shakspere in English! But I have never had the privilege of the gift of tongues, and I had to content myself with my own Italian, which is understood by but few in America. This, however, mattered little; they understood me all the same, or, to put it better, they caught by intuition my ideas and my sentiments.

My first appearance was in " Othello." The public received a strong impression, without discussing whether or not the means which I used to cause it were acceptable, and without forming a clear conception of my interpretation of that character, or pronouncing openly upon its form. The same people who had heard it the first night returned on the second, on the third, and even on the fourth, to make up their minds whether the emotions they experienced resulted from the novelty of my interpretation, or whether in fact it was the true sentiment of *Othello's* passions which was transmitted to them — in short, whether it was a mystification or a revelation. By degrees the public became convinced that those excesses of jealousy and fury were appropriate to the son of the desert, and that one of southern blood must be much better qualified to interpret them than a northerner. The judgment was discussed, criticized, disputed; but in the end the verdict was overwhelmingly in my favor. When the American has once said "Yes," he never weakens; he will always preserve for you the same esteem, sympathy, and affection. After New York I traveled through a number of American cities — Philadelphia, Baltimore, Pittsburg, Washington, and Boston, which is rightly styled the Athens of America, for there artistic taste is most refined. In Boston I had the good fortune to become intimately acquainted with the illustrious poet Longfellow, who talked to me in the pure Tuscan. I saw, too, other smaller cities, and then I appeared again in New York, where the favor of the public was confirmed, not only for me, but also for the artists of my company, and especially for Isolina Piamonti, who received no uncertain marks of esteem and consideration. We then proceeded to Albany, Utica, Syracuse, Rochester, Buffalo, Toledo, and that pleasant city, De-

troit, continuing to Chicago, and finally to
New Orleans. I reached New Orleans at
carnival time, and, in a masked procession in
which all nations were represented, I was
revolted and offended to see Italy figuring as
Pope Pius IX. giving his benediction to a
band of brigands, who with their daggers in
their teeth were kneeling at the Holy Father's
feet. I was so much disgusted by this offensive and repulsive travesty, due to the
suggestion of some renegade, as well as by
the unpardonable ignorance of the carnival
committee, that I could not refrain from publishing a letter of protest, over my signature,
in which I said:

Italy for true Italians should be represented by Victor
Emmanuel, by Gioberti, Cavour, and Garibaldi. Every
good Italian must repel, protest against, and despise this
insult offered to a nation which, by its antique traditions,
and by its recent deeds, deserves the respect and the admiration of the civilized world; and we are sure of finding
an echo of adhesion to this sentiment among the American
people, which is accustomed to render homage and justice
to all that is noble and generous.

Italians congratulated me, the press kept
silence, and the people remained indifferent;
and so the matter was forgotten. This was

the only disagreeable experience of this tour in America.

From New Orleans we sailed to Havana, but found in Cuba civil war, and a people that had but small appetite for serious things, and was moreover alarmed by a light outbreak of yellow fever. One of my company was taken down with the disease, but I had the pleasure of seeing him recover. Luckily he had himself treated by Havanese physicians, who are accustomed to combat that malady, which they know only too well. Perhaps my comrade would have lost his life under the ministrations of an Italian doctor. In the city of sugar and tobacco, too, it was "Othello" which carried off the palm. Those good manufacturers of cigars presented me on my benefit with boxes of their wares, which were made expressly for me, and which I despatched to Italy for the enjoyment of my friends. In spite of the many civilities which were tendered to me, in spite of considerable money profit, and of the ovations of its kind-hearted people, I did not find Cuba to my taste. Sloth and luxury reign there supreme.

I returned from Cuba to the United States,

and gave five performances in Philadelphia
and ten in New York, after which we went
to Rio de Janeiro on the steamer *Ontario*, a
voyage of twenty-eight days. We stopped
on the way at St. Thomas, and at Para, on
the great river Amazon. A short time after
our voyage, the *Ontario* was lost with all her
passengers and crew. My good star has always followed me, and in the innumerable
journeys undertaken during the long period
of my travels I have never had to lament an
accident.

AGAIN IN BRAZIL

THE Dom Pedro Theater of Rio de Janeiro
was the first scene of our activity. The au-
spicious season, the freedom from epidemic,
and the certain presence of the Emperor
Dom Pedro d'Alcantara, who had returned
from his travels in Europe, were most favorable, both to the brilliancy of our artistic
success, and to our financial profit. The
Emperor had me often at his palace in the
city, and invited me to a lunch at the country
palace of Petropolis, where I saw the Empress, to whom I could give no greater plea-

sure than to talk of her dear Naples. The
affability, kindness, and learning of Dom
Pedro are well known. He was a perfect
polyglot, and conversed with me in unim-
peachable Italian; the Empress still spoke
with the Neapolitan accent. I played ten
times at the Dom Pedro, and then I changed
to the Fluminense Theater, which was intended for opera, and there I appeared eight
times more, with a constantly growing afflu-
ence of spectators. On my days off, I enjoyed visiting the enchanting suburbs of the
city, and I formed the opinion that the real
America is in Brazil. There Nature bestows
her gifts with abundance, and all growth is
luxuriantly rank. The trees are as high as
our campanili, the roses are as large as pine-
apples, the birds display a thousand hues,
the sky is always serene, the men are courteous, the women most amiable, and even the
negroes are more docile and civilized than in
their native land. The climate, alas! leaves
much to be desired, and if a European is not
careful to lead a hygienic and well-regulated
life, he runs the risk of leaving his bones
there. I was under contract to go to Chile,
but during my stay in Brazil negotiations

11

were concluded arranging for a few appearances on the way at Montevideo, and at
Buenos Ayres. I gave twelve nights more
at Montevideo at the Solis Theater, for
which the house was taken by storm. For
my benefit the boxes and the best places
were put up at auction, and nearly twice the
proceeds of the regular prices was taken in.
The theater managers each made $2500 for
their own account. The people insisted upon
my remaining at Montevideo through all the
time that I had destined for Buenos Ayres,
and I consented the more readily because
in the latter city there was some appearance of political disturbance, which soon developed into civil war. The opera, which
had suspended at the Solis Theater to make
room for me, had to wait, under an in-
demnity, for two weeks more before opening again. I paid £1000 sterling to the
administration of the English steamers for
the voyage and return of my company from
Montevideo to Valparaiso, and, traversing
the Straits of Magellan, in eleven days we
were in Chile. I should not be frank if I
said that the Chileans received us with enthusiasm. Both at Valparaiso and at San-

tiago I had a *succès d'estime*, little more, and our business was light, but yet covered the large expenses of so costly a journey. The returns, however, did not compensate for the trouble of going there, especially as we were shut out of Peru by one of the numerous revolutions.

Upon my return I arranged to give a farewell appearance at Montevideo. On the morning of my arrival fourteen persons lay dead in the Plaza de la Matrice, as an accompaniment to the presidential elections. Our play was given, notwithstanding, and to a splendid house. This ended my engagements with the company, and I pursued the voyage on the same English steamer to Bordeaux, while my companions took the Italian ship.

APPEARANCE IN LONDON

In Paris I found a letter from the impresario Mapleson, who proposed that I should go to London with an Italian company, and play at Drury Lane on the off-nights of the opera. I was in doubt for a considerable time whether to challenge the verdict of the

British public; but in two weeks after reaching Italy, by dint of telegrams I had got together the force of artists necessary, and I presented myself with arms and baggage in London, in the spring of 1875.

Hardly had I arrived, when I noticed the posting, on the bill-boards of the city, of the announcement of the seventy-second night of "Hamlet" at the Lyceum Theater, with Henry Irving in the title rôle. I had contracted with Mapleson to give only three plays in my season, "Othello," the "Gladiator," and "Hamlet," the last having been insisted upon by Mapleson himself, who, as a speculator, well knew that curiosity as to a comparison would draw the public to Drury Lane.

IMPRESSIONS OF IRVING'S "HAMLET"

I WAS very anxious to see the illustrious English artist in that part, and I secured a box and went to the Lyceum. I was recognized by nobody, and remaining as it were concealed in my box, I had a good opportunity to satisfy my curiosity. I arrived at the theater a little too late, so that I missed the

scene of *Hamlet* in presence of the ghost of
his father—the scene which in my judgment
contains the clue to that strange character,
and from which all the synthetic ideas of
Hamlet are developed. I was in time to hear
only the last words of the oath of secrecy. I
was struck by the perfection of the stage
setting. There was a perfect imitation of the
effect of moonlight, which at the proper times
flooded the stage with its rays or left it in
darkness. Every detail was excellently and
exactly reproduced. The scene was shifted,
and *Hamlet* began his allusions, his sallies of
sarcasm, his sententious sayings, his points
of satire with the courtiers who sought to
study and to penetrate the sentiments of the
young prince. In this scene Irving was
simply sublime. His mobile face mirrored
his thoughts. The subtle penetration of his
phrases, so perfect in shading and incisiveness, showed him to be a master of art. I do
not believe there is an actor who can stand
beside him in this respect, and I was so much
impressed by it, that at the end of the second
act I said to myself, "I will not play *Hamlet!*
Mapleson can say what he likes, but I will
not play it"; and I said it with the fullest

11*

resolution.   In the monologue, "To be, or
not to be," Irving was admirable; in the
scene with *Ophelia* he was deserving of the
highest praise; in that of the *Players* he was
moving, and in all this part of the play he appeared to my eyes to be the most perfect
interpreter of that eccentric character.   But
further on it was not so, and for the sake of
art I regretted it.   From the time when the
passion assumes a deeper hue, and reasoning
moderates impulses which are forcibly curbed,
Irving seemed to me to show mannerism, and
to be lacking in power, and strained; and it is
not in him alone that I find this fault, but in
nearly all foreign actors.   There seems to be
a limit of passion within which they remain
true in their rendering of nature; but beyond
that limit they become transformed, and take
on conventionality in their intonations, exaggeration in their gestures, and mannerism in
their bearing.   I left my box saying to myself, "I too can do *Hamlet*, and I will try
it!"   In some characters Irving is exception-
ally fine.   I am convinced that it would be
difficult to interpret *Shylock* or *Mephistopheles*
better than he.   He is most skilful in putting
his productions on the stage; and in addition

to his intelligence he does not lack the power
to communicate his counsels or his teachings.
Withal he is an accomplished gentleman in
society, and is loved and respected by his fellow-citizens, who justly look upon him as a
glory to their country. He should, however,
for his own sake, avoid playing such parts as
Romeo and *Macbeth*, which are not adapted
to his somewhat scanty physical and vocal
power.

THE DECLINE OF TRAGEDY

THE traditions of the English drama are
imposing and glorious! Shakspere alone has
gained the highest pinnacle of fame in dramatic art. He has had to interpret him such
great artists as Garrick, Kemble, Kean, Ma-
cready, Siddons, and Irving; and the literary
and dramatic critics of the whole world have
studied and analyzed both author and actors.
At present, however, tragedy is abandoned
on almost all the stages of Europe. Actors
who devote themselves to tragedy, whether
classical, romantic, or historical, no longer
exist. Society comedy has overflowed the
stage, and the inundation causes the seed to

rot which more conscientious and prudent
planters had sown in the fields of art. It is
desirable that the feeling and taste for the
works of the great dramatists should be re-
vived in Europe, and that England, which is
for special reasons, and with justice, proud of
enjoying the primacy in dramatic composition,
should have also worthy and famous actors.
I do not understand why the renown and
prestige of the great name of Garrick do not
attract modern actors to follow in his foot-
steps. Do not tell me that the works of
Shakspere are out of fashion, and that the
public no longer wants them. Shakspere is
always new—so new that not even yet is he
understood by everybody; and if, as they say,
the public is no longer attracted by his plays,
it is because they are superficially presented.
To win the approval of the audience, a dazzling and conspicuous *mise en scène* does not
suffice, as some seem to imagine, to make up
deficiency in interpretation ; a more profound
study of the characters represented is indispensable. If in art you can join the beautiful
and the good, so much the better for you ;
but if you give the public the alternative, it
will always prefer the good to the beautiful.

RECEPTION IN LONDON

My season in London was a real event. The London public had very great attractions both at Drury Lane and at Covent Garden. At the former such celebrated artists as Nilsson and Tietjens, with the tenors Campanini and Fancelli, and the basso Nannetti, were singing in "Lohengrin," "Fidelio," and "Lucia di Lammermoor"; at Covent Garden, Patti and the barytone Cotogni were delighting their hearers with "La Traviata," "Dinorah," and the "Barbiere di Siviglia." I was acting at Drury Lane on the three alternate nights when opera was not given. Whether it was the novelty, or that "Othello" had not been played for a long time, or merely one of the anomalies of the public, which, when it has once set its face in any direction, can with difficulty be made to change, Drury Lane was crowded on the nights when I played *Othello*. The Prince of Wales did me the honor to summon me to his box to assure me of his admiration. The celebrated poet Browning proved his friendship by securing my admission as a guest to the Athenæum Club. The Garrick Club and the Arts Club tendered me a reception, and granted me honorary membership. I went to call upon the *diva* Patti, who was surrounded by the most select society, on one of her reception-days, and she had the courtesy to make me this compliment: "Do you know, Salvini, that I am a little jealous of you?"

Between April 1 and July 16, 1875, I gave "Othello" thirty times, the "Gladiator" four times, and "Hamlet" on my last ten appearances. The last play gave the final touch to my reputation; to this a few lines which I had from Robert Browning will testify. After playing *Hamlet* I expressed to him my regret that I had not been able to attain in that rôle all that I had aimed at; and he answered me:

My DEAR SALVINI: I do not know whether what you say to me is true about the chords of tenderness which you lacked, or which failed to respond to the touch, in your first representation of "Hamlet." But this I know, that during your play on Friday the entire lyre of tragedy resounded magnificently. Ever yours,

ROBERT BROWNING.

I left behind in London many genial acquaintances and enduring friendships, besides a sincere affection for a young orphan girl who became my wife in the course of that year. I went away with much regret, but with the hope of returning to England for the long season of the following year.

A TOUR OF GREAT BRITAIN

I RETURNED to Italy well satisfied with my first experience in London, and I arranged with Colonel Mapleson for a tour in England to begin March 1, 1876, to include the chief cities outside of London, and the season in the capital itself. My new wife was unable to accompany me on the journey which had previously been arranged, and she remained in Florence. I visited Newcastle, Manchester, Liverpool, Edinburgh, Glasgow, Dublin, Belfast, and Birmingham, and on May 15 I appeared again in London, at the Queen's Theater, which has since been pulled down. Mr. Mapleson certainly was not fortunate in his choice of so obscure a theater; yet our performance of "Othello" drew, even if under difficulties, a public generous of applause. After the seventh repetition of the Moor of Venice I fell seriously ill, tortured

by a carbuncle between the shoulder-blades,
which gave me intense suffering.   For seventeen days I could not close my eyes, and
when wearied nature could no longer resist
sleep, the lancinating spasms of my torment
counterbalanced the refreshment.   The Prince
of Wales showed me the thoughtful attention of sending me his own physician, who
after consultation declared that my days were
numbered.   Fortunately he was mistaken ;
but the gloomy opinion spread, and several
newspapers mentioned it.   My sole anxiety
was the fear that it would reach my wife's
ears; and to prevent her from setting out to
join me, and spare her the fatigues of the
journey and a great anxiety, which would
surely have been injurious to her in her condition, I sent her word that a severe attack
of rheumatism in my right shoulder pre-
vented me from writing to her with my own
hand.   In this state of affairs I saw that even
if I were to get well I should be an invalid
for several months, and I determined to discharge my company and shoulder the financial loss.   Although my doctor sought to
console me with hopeful words, from the impression betrayed by my dear and good

friends who came to see me, I was convinced that all was over with me. Some of
them had hardly entered the room and
caught sight of me, when they fled without
speaking, covering their eyes with their
hands, and making other manifestations of
grief.

Fate willed that my illness should gradually assume a less alarming character; and
after three days, during which I was given
up, the doctor declared that the danger was
past, but that I should have to undergo, as
I had anticipated, a long convalescence. My
appetite returned a little, I was able to keep
up my strength with good wine, and soon
I was assured that I should live to see again
my family and my native land. As soon as
I could stand on my feet, I arranged everything for my departure. I stopped for two
days in Paris to rest. Ristori, who was stay-
ing in that capital with her family, had previously invited me to spend a day with her,
and she was astonished at my emaciation
and at the alteration in my features. When
at last I reached Florence, I had to explain
everything to my wife, who gave herself up
to a torrent of tears at the thought of my

danger, and of how she had been cut off from succoring me in this painful experience.

VIENNA

AFTER a period of rest with my family at San Marcello and Antiguano, I returned to Florence with my health perfectly regained, and with all my former energy, and formed a new company with the purpose of going to Austria and Germany. To secure the applause of a public accustomed to weigh in the balance artists as conscientious, as thoughtful, and as philosophic as the Germans was a prize not to be despised, and I desired to win it. On February 22, 1877, I opened at the Ring Theater in Vienna, with the indispensable "Othello"; and although the audience, with a few exceptions, did not understand a word I uttered, I flattered myself that I was received with favor. This confusion of tongues, which, as we are taught, God brought about as a punishment upon the builders of the Tower of Babel, might, one would think, be revoked after so many years, so that all might use one language. But this is not to be! To-day every ignorant person speaks one language; one who respects himself must be master of two; an educated man must know three or four; and a learned man is necessarily a polyglot. Yet it seems to me that all the time that must be spent in the study of language is wasted, and that it could be given much more fruitfully to the acquisition of the sciences. I envy those who can learn many tongues with ease, for this gift has never developed in me; and in Vienna, particularly, because of this, I suffered some embarrassment. We Italians have, however, a facility in making ourselves understood without speaking, supplying the lack of words by gestures, and by the mobility of our expression, and by these means I was often able to unravel difficulties. The most lively interest in my playing was shown by the artists of the Burg Theater, some of whom I had the pleasure of knowing intimately; and I shall always cherish the recollection of the courtesies which I received from Sonnenthal, Lewinsky, Mitterwusser, and the clever and amiable wife of the last. The Viennese are full of enthusiasm for the arts; they honor and appreciate highly any one who rises above mediocrity, and give expression to their sentiments by the nightly homage to their favorite artists of a profusion of flowers and wreaths. I made such a collection of souvenirs that my lodgings were hardly large enough to hold them all. The press was unusually favorable to me, and from the translations which I procured of the articles concerning me I found that little or nothing had escaped appreciation of all that I had expected would be lost on account of my foreign idiom. I do not refer to the praises which were addressed to me, but to the detailed studies of my conceptions. There were just observations, judgments seriously weighed, urbane and dignified criticisms, and praise unmarred by exaggeration : nothing could be more correct, more wise, more conscientious.

The German actors have one most valuable quality—that of studying much, a feature which in general is wanting in us Italians, for we are wont to fancy that we have done much study when in fact our preparation is still insufficient. The Germans are more patient in application; they investigate

CLEMENTINA CAZZOLA.

with accuracy the personage whom they are to play, and they lead all the actors of the world in their talent for merging their own personality in that of their rôle. It may be that they are somewhat lacking in life, that they do not rise to the feverish heights of passion, but always remain calm and collected; but what harmony and precision in the whole! One might imagine that they were guided by a mathematical study, as it were, of their art, and that they had undertaken to put it into methodical practice. From this come that unison, that evenness of the whole, which have earned such high encomiums for the Meininger Company. The great actress Wolter, the Ristori of the North, by her intellectual qualities stands in the first rank among the actresses of the century. In talent and penetration, and in identification of herself with her rôles, she is second to none, and she is not wanting in a spark of genius to illuminate her carefully elaborated interpretations.

I remained at Vienna from February 22 to April 8, and played twenty-five times in "Othello," "Hamlet," "Macbeth," the "Gladiator," the "Morte Civile," "David

Garrick," and "Ingomar." I made the acquaintance of the author of the last very beautiful and interesting composition, Baron von Bellinhausen, who wrote under the pseudonym of F. Halm, and he was kind enough to declare me his most successful interpreter. If you can only succeed in an enterprise, your temerity in having attempted it will always be condoned; and it was in truth a temerity on my part to play in Vienna a German piece which had already been admirably presented by celebrated actors. But "fortune favors the brave!"

A RECITATION AT DOM PEDRO'S

DURING my season in Vienna, Dom Pedro d'Alcantara, Emperor of Brazil, and the most erudite crowned head of the century, was expected in that city. One morning at eight o'clock the secretary of the Brazilian legation came to my hotel to announce to me that the Emperor Dom Pedro desired to see me as soon as possible. I dressed at once, and at nine I was in the presence of his Majesty. As soon as he saw me he said to me in pure Italian, and with as much eagerness as if he were asking me to save his throne: "Salvini, you must do me a service!" I was somewhat taken aback, for I did not see how I could be in a position to do service to an emperor. "Your Majesty," I said, "in what can I be so happy as to serve you?" He answered: "You must play the 'Morte Civile.'" I was reassured and breathed freely, and answered: "It will give me much pleasure, your Majesty; but I have already given the 'Morte Civile' five times, and I fear that the public may have had enough of it." "Do it the sixth time for me," said the Emperor, "and never mind the public." I said: "Your Majesty's judgment outbalances that of an entire public, and your desire shall be satisfied as an honor to myself." On that evening all aristocratic Austria crowded the Ring Theater. During Dom Pedro's sojourn in Vienna, I was invited to recite Prati's poem "La Cena d'Alboino," in a large concert-hall, for the benefit of the Viennese students. In addition the entertainment consisted of vocal and instrumental music. Dom Pedro was among the first of the audience to arrive. While I was waiting my turn, an aide-de-camp of the Emperor Francis

Joseph invited Dom Pedro to go to the imperial palace on some pressing business. Dom
Pedro was visibly annoyed, but he arose and
left the hall, so I had to make my recitation
without him as an auditor.   Before he left
Vienna, being unable to return all the innumerable attentions paid to him, he directed his
minister to give a grand entertainment, and I
was not forgotten.   Unfortunately I had to
play *Othello* on the night in question. Greatly
fatigued as I always was by that play, when
it was done I dressed, and went to the Brazilian minister's residence. The crowd of no-
bles and dignitaries, with all the feminine
aristocracy of Vienna, was so dense as to
make it almost impossible to pass from one
room to another.   I placed myself in a door-
way, and perceived Dom Pedro before me,
who, while talking with the Princess Metter-
nich, kept turning his glance in my direction.
Of a sudden he rose, and, coming straight up
to me, he requested me to repeat the poem of
Prati's of which he was so fond, and which he
had been unable to hear at the Academy.   I
saw that I was lost.

"Your Majesty," said I, "I come from
playing *Othello*, and my voice is rough from

it; moreover, I do not know whether it will be opportune for me to recite in Italian before these ladies and gentlemen who are not acquainted with the language."

"Never mind! Never mind!" he replied. "If these gentlemen do not understand, so much the worse for them; but you will do me a very great pleasure, for I am very fond of those verses of Prati's, whom I know personally."

How could I refuse? Soon the orchestra, which had been playing on a raised dais, passed into another room, and the dais was left free for my stage. Dom Pedro himself directed the placing of chairs in rows like those of a theater; and when all was ready, and the company had been informed of what I was to recite, the Emperor invited me to begin. I found that not all my audience were ignorant of Italian, for from time to time there were spontaneous cries of *Bravo!* and *Bene!* Some understood, some pretended to understand, and most understood not a word. My recitation was nevertheless effective, and when it was done I was surrounded by many beautiful ladies and by many gentlemen, who offered me abundant

12*

congratulations—perhaps to pay their court
to the Emperor. Dom Pedro waited until
the crowd had finished its phrases of admiration, and then approached me, much moved,
and spoke in my ear only the words: "Sublime! Thank you." This was at about two
o'clock, and I drove back to my lodgings so
wearied and worn out that I could not sleep,
by reason of my overwrought nerves. The
next day I concluded that it was at no little
sacrifice that one could win the admiration
of an emperor. I ought, however, to be
grateful to him, for after such an advertise-
ment the Ring Theater was patronized by
the best society during the remaining nights
of my season.

PLAYING AT POTSDAM

From Vienna I went to Pesth, thence to
Prague, and then to Berlin. In the capital
of Germany I met with a flattering greeting.
I had the opportunity to know the most distinguished men in literature and in art. The
court displayed much interest in my acting,
and the old Emperor William particularly, as

I judged, must have felt much sympathy for me, for he would rise from his chair and go to the back of his box to applaud without being seen. It appears that etiquette imposed upon him reserve in open manifestation of approval. The Crown-princess Victoria, now the widow of the Emperor Frederick, honored me with undisguised marks of her approval, and did not lose a single one of my performances. People wanted me to petition for presentation at court, but I declined, for the reason that I did not care to expose myself to the humiliation of a refusal, and that if any of the august personages desired to know me personally, they had only to command my presence before them. It seemed that etiquette did not admit of that; but my feeling of delicacy kept me fixed in my resolution. At last I received a summons to present myself at court. I was received by the Crown-prince Frederick William and the Crown-princess Victoria, with all their children, then very small, and was treated with the greatest affability and courtesy. Among many questions which they put to me, they asked me whether I should have any objection to give a play with my company in the theater at

Potsdam. I could not refuse so kindly an
invitation. The evening and the play were
decided upon. The next day a chamberlain
came to ask me diplomatically what compensation I wished for giving this play at the
private court theater. I answered that when
I gave my coöperation for an entertainment
outside of a public theater it was not my
custom to fix a price, and that I would not
do it. The chamberlain, however, insisted,
saying that it was not proper that the court
should accept a gift; to which I replied that
it was not my intention to make a gift, and
that I would ask as my compensation the
gloves which the Crown-princess would have
worn when applauding me. I had great
trouble to persuade the diplomatic messenger
to take back my answer, but he had to content himself with it. On the appointed day
I took my company to Potsdam to play
"Sullivan," a comedy for which only the
dress of to-day is requisite. All my actors
were lodged in a wing of the palace, where
refreshments were provided, and I was invited to take my place in a carriage in which
were the Crown-princess Victoria and her
sons, and we drove to Sans Souci to visit

the memorials to Frederick the Great and to Voltaire. The Princess described every object and locality to me in detail, with the greatest interest and affability, together with all the memories attached to scenes so full of associations. Upon our return to the palace, I made ready to give my play. A sudden indisposition kept the old Emperor from being present. The small but graceful theater was literally packed with the official representatives of all nations, with the most distinguished of the nobility, the diplomatic corps, the magistracy, and the military. The performance was of glacial frigidity, for at court all applause is absolutely prohibited. After the play I was invited to take tea with the Crown-prince and Crown-princess, and I found myself in the midst of all these beautiful and elegant ladies and distinguished gentlemen, who plied me with questions, congratulations, and compliments. Of these one, which surpassed all the others both in its form and in its exquisite idea, was addressed to me by the Crown-princess, who said to me: "Since Rachel, you are the first, Salvini, to tread the stage at Potsdam; I think that its doors must be closed after so great an event!" And in fact

the doors of the theater in Potsdam have not
been reopened since my appearance there. I
went away from Berlin delighted with the
kindness and courtesy of the German court,
and with a public of such intelligence; and
upon my arrival at Trieste, where I stopped
to make four appearances, I was informed
by the German consul that there was an object addressed to me at the custom-house. I
went there, and found a ring with a solitaire
diamond which had been sent to me by the
Emperor William and the Crown-prince and
Crown-princess, as a souvenir of my appearance at Potsdam.

A SECOND VISIT TO PARIS

My company was still engaged for the
whole month of June, and I wished to take
advantage of the opportunity to appear four
times at Venice. The Princess Margherita
of Savoy, now our beloved queen, was at
Venice for the sea-bathing, and was present
at all my performances. I preserve pre-
ciously a beautiful souvenir which she was
good enough to send me. From Venice I

returned to Florence, and again took up my wanderings with different actors and actresses. I opened at Paris, October 3, 1877, in the Salle Ventadour; of all that I played there, to the "Morte Civile" was adjudged the palm. It was a real revelation to the Parisians. It would be tedious to repeat all that the greatest artistic and literary luminaries wrote of it. Victor Hugo, La Pommeraye, Zola, Gautier, Vitu, elevated to the stars both composition and interpretation. The celebrated dramatic critic Vitu even made a translation of it, so that it might be acted in French at the Odéon. Not "Othello," not "Macbeth," not "Ingomar," nothing aroused such interest as Paolo Giacometti's drama.

After three nights at Antwerp, six at Brussels, and two at Lille, I went back to Paris for eleven more, five of which were devoted to the "Morte Civile."

ESTIMATE OF MOUNET-SULLY

In Paris I had the opportunity to know the famous Mounet-Sully, whom I admired much in Victor Hugo's "Hernani," and to whom I

permitted myself to make a small criticism
on his highly artistic and meritorious performance—a criticism of the justice of which
he was fully convinced.   It is only conscientious artists who are able to recognize their
own defects.   I found in Mounet-Sully too
much nervousness; he was always on the
stretch, continually in forced action, as if
something might break at any moment.   He
was a man of fine presence, of most accurate
delivery, and if he could have freed himself
from the traditions imposed upon him by the
Conservatory,—traditions to which all French
actors who adopt the serious style are subjected,—it would have aided him to be less
conventional.   He is to-day one of the most
solid pillars of the Maison de Molière, and
that is not a little thing.

SARAH BERNHARDT

ONE night when I went on the stage to
see Mounet-Sully he presented me to Mme.
Sarah Bernhardt.   I had never heard that
excellent artist except as *Doña Sol* in "Hernani."   I was entirely satisfied with her physical and vocal gifts, as well as with her incisive

and penetrating diction, but it seemed to me that her movements were a little angular. I saw her another time in the "Dame aux Camélias," and she was attractive in the earlier acts, both from her "voice of gold," as the French style it, and from the naturalism with which she molded the character. At some points I noted a little precipitation in her delivery, the reason for which I had not observed in Victor Hugo's verses; and while I recognized in her superior talent for assuming her rôle and modulating the various expressions of the voice, for so accentuating her phrases as to give them brilliancy, and for making herself up with that attractiveness which is, perhaps, peculiar to French actresses, yet I could not help noticing, especially in the last act of the play, a seeking after effects that were discordant with the position and character of the personage. I saw her afterward at Florence in Sardou's "La Tosca," and in that play she produced the same effect on me. She has very great gifts, an exceptional artistic quality, and notable defects. When I went through Paris on my last return from North America, I saw her in "Jeanne d'Arc."

I am not blind to the fascinating merits of

that eccentric actress, and I proclaim her the
brightest star which has in recent years risen
above the horizon of dramatic art; but I ask,
is the superiority attributed to her by the
world all pure gold? Is there not in it a taint
of alloy?   Her sentiment, her artistic intuition, the acuteness of her interpretation,
her moving and harmonious voice, the just
accentuation of her phrasing, the tastefulness
of her dress—all this is gold, pure gold.   A
slight tendency to declamation, a use of gesticulation not always appropriate, a marked
precipitation of speech, especially at critical
moments, and a pronounced monotony in pa-
thetic expression, constitute the alloy.   So
much has been, and is still, said of the extrav-
agances of that original genius, that wherever
she goes, no one will stay away from seeing
her.   It must, however, be admitted that all
these advertisements draw more attention to
the woman than to the actress.

COQUELIN

I must give, too, my impression of another
celebrated French artist, an impression which

is highly favorable to him, yet not without a
" but," for which he will bear me no grudge.
He is the cleverest, the most exact, the most
delicate, the most keen in his delivery of a
monologue that our century has produced.
Every one has already perceived that I refer to the elder Coquelin.   How subtle and
bright is the intelligence which this actor
brings into play to give life to his delivery!
With how artistic a touch he colors every period, every phrase!   In how just a measure
he balances his effects, so insinuating his
humorous anecdotes that one would fancy
they were told by many persons and not by
himself alone!   The variety of his voice, the
mobility of his face, are powerful auxiliaries,
which he uses with studied art; he is never
vulgar, never artificial, never monotonous,
never incorrect.   If this almost perfect artist
could disabuse himself in the matter of playing a few parts which are not adapted either
to his natural tendencies or to his characteristic face, if he would confine himself to such
typical characters as do not have to support
the responsibility of the entire play, in my
opinion he would heighten his fame.   When
one does everything, one does too much, and

can with difficulty attain to perfection. For
that matter, this fault is found in many great
artists, and I have seen but rare exceptions.

THE FRENCH PUBLIC

WHAT can I say of the French public?
Has it a taste of its own, an independent
judgment? I doubt it. Those ten, twenty,
and thirty men of superior intelligence who
never miss a first night, whether of music or
drama, guide and lead after them the mass
of the audience. Would the claque with its
paid applause ever have become established
in France if the public had an opinion of its
own? And if it had such an opinion, would
it submit to the imposition of judgment upon
it? It is very true that if the play or the
actor is not in touch with the audience, the
claque has not the power to force it to return
and see the same play, but it serves, nevertheless, to modify any distaste on the part of
the public. In Italy it could have no other
effect than to make the public still more
hostile to a play. One can never obtain
a sincere, independent, legitimate judgment

from the mass of the French public. If the thirty intelligent persons do not approve, the mass will remain indifferent. And just so it is with the press. If the papers favor a play, they have much influence on public opinion, they incite the people to fill the theater, and the audience, whether it will or no, is persuaded that it has been amused. If the censors are unfavorable, the house will stay empty. Hence it results that it is never the public which decides, but the thirty assiduous men of intelligence who render the verdict, and the press which condemns or applauds.

When I was again in Florence, I lived quietly and happily with my wife, whom I could not take with me on my professional tours, since she was obliged to attend to our family affairs, and to care as well for her own health. During the summer I busied myself with my garden and vineyard on my small property near Florence. At the end of October, 1879, we returned to our winter quarters in Florence, and on November 13 our second child was born, after which event my wife was taken with an obstinate fever; then inflammation set in, and finally scarlet fever, which in her enfeebled condition did not break

13

out openly, but none the less accomplished
its maleficent work.   After a month of suffering under this accumulation of ills, a violent
attack of peritonitis developed, and the poor
creature, worn out, lost her reason and then
her life, leaving me two little babies as
memorials of our love.

I cannot describe my anguish of mind.
The world imagines that the artist wraps up
all his aspirations in his own self-love. It is
indeed true that that satisfaction appeals to
the mind, but it cannot compensate for the
tortures of the heart. Not to have known
my mother, who died when I was two years
old; to have lost my father at fifteen; to have
seen waste away, still young, the woman who
first inspired me with deep affection; to have
been bereaved of my wife, who was not yet
twenty-four; and finally, to see a brother die
upon whom I had counted as the friend of
my old age—all this I have endured.   Truly
those who have no feelings are most happy!

A TOUR OF EASTERN EUROPE

LEFT alone by the death of my wife, with
my well-grown sons at school, and my last

children too young to give me any consola-
tion, I threw myself with renewed ardor into
the embrace of art, resolved to seek no other
distraction, but to look for relief and oblivion
in unwearied study, in practice on the stage,
in continuous traveling; but throughout four
years it was impossible for me to forget my
misfortune. All that was not connected with
my art was repulsive to me: to new acquain-
tanceships I was indifferent; traveling did not
cheer me; and even in the exercise of my
profession the dominating recollection of the
irreparable loss I had suffered remained fixed
in my mind.

On November 11, 1879, I again started
out, this time for Trieste, whence I went
again to Vienna. Having given a few nights
at Pesth, I went on to the cosmopolitan city
of Russia, Odessa. There everybody has
a more or less complete knowledge of Italian,
and I had a festive greeting from the hetero-
geneous population.

I remained in Odessa from January 15 to
February 20, 1880, and then went to Roumania, where I first appeared on February
23. I played six times at Jassy, three times
at Galatz, twice at Braila, and finally, on
March 20, I proceeded to the capital, and

stayed there until April 14. I was so well
received by the people and their rulers, that
the Prince, now King Charles I., honored
me with the Star of Roumania. The schol-
arly Princess, now Queen Pauline Elizabeth
("Carmen Sylva"), showed me the greatest
kindness and courtesy. She had the kindness to read to me one of her poetical works,
written in French, which seemed to me full
of dash and interest, and elegant in form. I
shall always retain an agreeable memory of
the exquisite welcome of that court. After
leaving Bucharest I played three times at
Cracow, and on April 20 left Roumania to return to Florence, in order to take breath for
my future peregrinations.

TRAGEDY IN TWO LANGUAGES

In this year the agent of an impresario and
theater-owner of Boston came to Florence to
make me the proposal that I should go to
North America for the second time, to play
in Italian supported by an American company. I thought the man had lost his senses.
But after a time I became convinced that he
was in his right mind, and that no one would

undertake a long and costly journey simply to play a joke, and I took his extraordinary proposition into serious consideration, and asked him for explanations.

"The idea is this," the agent made answer; "it is very simple. You found favor the last time with the American public with your Italian company, when not a word that was said was understood, and the proprietor of the Globe Theater of Boston thinks that if he puts with you English-speaking actors, you will yourself be better understood, since all the dialogue of your supporters will be plain. The audience will concern itself only with following you, with the aid of the play-books in both languages, and will not have to pay any attention to the others, whose words it will understand."

"But how shall I take my cue, since I do not understand English? And how will your American actors know when to speak, since they do not know Italian?"

"Have no anxiety about that," said the agent. "Our American actors are mathematicians, and can memorize perfectly the last words of your speeches, and they will work with the precision of machines."

13*

" I am ready to admit that," said I, " although I do not think it will be so easy; but
it will in any case be much easier for them,
who will have to deal with me alone, and will
divide the difficulty among twenty or twenty-
four, than for me, who must take care of.all."

The persevering agent, however, closed
my mouth with the words, " You do not sign
yourself ' Salvini ' for nothing!"   He had an
answer for everything, he was prepared to
convince me at all points, to persuade me
about everything, and to smooth over every
difficulty, and he won a consent which,
though almost involuntary on my part, was
legalized by a contract in due form, by which
I undertook to be at New York not later
than November 15, 1880, and to be ready to
open at Philadelphia with " Othello" on the
29th of the same month.

I was still dominated by my bereavement,
and the thought was pleasant to me of going
away from places which constantly brought
it back to my mind.   Another sky, other
customs, another language, grave responsi-
bilities, a novel and difficult undertaking of
uncertain outcome—I was willing to risk all
simply to distract my attention and to forget.

I have never in my life been a gambler, but that time I staked my artistic reputation upon a single card. Failure would have been a new emotion, severe and grievous, it is true, but still different from that which filled my mind. I played, and I won! The friends whom I had made in the United States in 1873, and with whom I had kept up my acquaintance, when they learned of the confusion of tongues, wrote me discouraging letters. In Italy the thing was not believed, so eccentric did it seem. I arrived in New York nervous and feverish, but not discouraged or depressed.

When the day of the first rehearsal came, all the theaters were occupied, and I had to make the best of a rather large concert-hall to try to get in touch with the actors who were to support me. An Italian who was employed in a newspaper-office served me as interpreter in coöperation with the agent of my Boston impresario. The American artists began the rehearsal without a prompter, and with a sureness to be envied especially by our Italian actors, who usually must have every word suggested to them. My turn came, and the few words which *Othello* pro-

nounces in the first scene came in smoothly
and without difficulty.   When the scene with
the *Council of Ten* came, of a sudden I could
not recall the first line of a paragraph, and I
hesitated; I began a line, but it was not that;
I tried another with no better success; a
third, but the interpreter told me that I had
gone wrong.   We began again, but the English was of no assistance to me in recognizing
which of my speeches corresponded to that
addressed to me, which I did not understand.
I was all at sea, and I told the interpreter to
beg the actors to overlook my momentary
confusion, and to say to them that I should
be all right in five minutes.   I went off to a
corner of the hall and bowed my head between my hands, saying to myself, "I have
come for this, and I must carry it through."
I set out to number mentally all the para-
graphs of my part, and in a short time I said,
" Let us begin again."

During the remainder of the rehearsal one
might have thought that I understood English, and that the American actors understood
Italian.   No further mistake was made by
either side; there was not even the smallest
hesitation, and when I finished the final scene

of the third act between *Othello* and *Iago*, the actors applauded, filled with joy and pleasure. The exactitude with which the subsequent rehearsals of "Othello," and those of "Hamlet," proceeded was due to the memory, the application, and the scrupulous attention to their work of the American actors, as well as to my own force of will and practical acquaintance with all the parts of the play, and to the natural intuition which helped me to know without understanding what was addressed to me, divining it from a motion, a look, or a light inflection of the voice. Gradually a few words, a few short phrases, remained in my ear, and in course of time I came to understand perfectly every word of all the characters; I became so sure of myself that if an actor substituted one word for another I perceived it. I understood the words of Shakspere, but not those of the spoken language.

In a few days we went to Philadelphia to begin our representations. My old acquaintances were in despair. To those who had sought to discourage me by their letters others on the spot joined their influence, and tried everything to overthrow my courage. I

must admit that the nearer came the hour of
the great experiment, the more my anxiety
grew, and inclined me to deplore the moment
when I had put myself in that dilemma. I
owe it in a great degree to my cool head that
my discouraging forebodings did not unman
me so much as to make me abandon myself
wholly to despair. Just as I was going on
the stage, I said to myself: "After all, what
can happen to me? They will not murder
me. I shall have tried, and I shall have
failed; that is all there will be to it. I will
pack up my baggage and go back to Italy,
convinced that oil and wine will not mix."
A certain contempt of danger, a firm resolution to succeed, and, I am bound to add, considerable confidence in myself, enabled me to
go before the public calm, bold, and secure.

The first scene before the palace of *Brabantio* was received with sepulchral silence.
When that of the *Council of Ten* came, and
the narration of the vicissitudes of *Othello*
was ended, the public broke forth in prolonged applause. Then I said to myself:
"A good beginning is half the work." At
the close of the first act, my adversaries, who
were such solely on account of their love of

art, and their belief that the two languages could not be amalgamated, came on the stage to embrace and congratulate me, surprised, enchanted, enthusiastic, happy that they had been mistaken, and throughout the play I was the object of constant demonstrations of sympathy.

AMERICAN CRITICAL TASTE

From Philadelphia we went to New York, where our success was confirmed. It remained for me to win the suffrages of Boston, and I secured them, first having made stops in Brooklyn, New Haven, and Hartford. When in the American Athens I became convinced that that city possesses the most refined artistic taste. The theatrical audiences are serious, attentive to details, analytical,—I might almost say scientific,—and one might fancy that such careful critics had never in their lives done anything but occupy themselves with scenic art. With reference to a presentation of Shakspere, they are profound, acute, subtile, and they know so well how to clothe some traditional principle in close logic, that if faith in the opposite is not

quite unshakable in an artist, he must feel
himself tempted to renounce his own tenets.
It is surprising that in a land where industry
and commerce seem to absorb all the intelligence of the people, there should be in every
city and district, indeed in every village, people who are competent to discuss the arts
with such high authority. The American
nation counts only a century of freedom, yet
it has produced a remarkable number of men
of high competence in dramatic art. Those
who think of tempting fortune by displaying
their untried artistic gifts on the American
stage, counting on the ignorance or inexperi-
ence of their audience, make a very unsafe
calculation. The taste and critical faculty of
that public are in their fullness of vigor.
Old Europe is more bound by traditions,
more weary, more *blasé*, in her judgment, not
always sincere or disinterested. In America the national pride is warmly felt, and
the national artists enjoy high honor. The
Americans know how to offer an exquisite
hospitality, but woe to the man who seeks
to impose on them! They profess a cult, a
veneration, for those who practise our art,
whether of their own nation or foreign, and

their behavior in the theater is dignified. I recall one night when upon invitation I went to see a new play in which appeared an actor of reputation. The play was not liked, and from act to act I noticed that the house grew more and more scanty, like a faded rose which loses its petals one by one, until at the last scene my box was the only one which remained occupied. I was more impressed by this silent demonstration of hostility than I should have been if the audience had made a tumultuous expression of its disapproval. The actors were humiliated and confounded, and as the curtain fell an instinctive sentiment of compassion induced me to applaud.

To return to my tour. From Boston I went to Montreal and Toronto, thence to Cincinnati for a week, and again to New York for a fortnight. I think that all my dramatic colleagues will agree with me that the life of an actor in America is extremely wearing. The system obtains everywhere of opening the theaters every night, and I cannot blame the owners from the point of view of their own interests; for since they hire their watchmen and attendants by the year, they must pay their salaries whether their

houses are open or closed. They are therefore constrained to impose similar conditions
upon the managers. The most celebrated
artists must therefore play every night except
Sunday, and in some States even on that day,
and on one or two days of the week they
must play twice. Think of an artist, all of
whose repertory is made up of tragedies of
Shakspere, and tell me whether it is possible
that human strength can resist such a strain.

Admitting that one's nerves may be elastic
enough to endure it, one cannot control the
vocal organs; and after a few weeks of such
exaggerated effort, the actor's strength and
vocal faculty diminish, and the later representations seem pale, and without the life and
fire required for the best results. I always
held back from submitting myself to this imposition; I was never willing to play more
than four or at the most five times a week,
and even to the injury of my immediate interests I would never depart from this resolution. There may have been actors able to
support the burden more easily, but I know,
though endowed with muscles of steel, sound
health, and a strong voice, I would not undertake it. I know well that to keep a

machine in good running order, there must
be time to keep it always polished and oiled;
with this precaution, even after fifty years of
activity, it will not show a trace of rust, and
will still be in condition to perform its regular
functions. In so long a period my machine
was forced to stop only twice; and both
times, after the damage was repaired,— damage which resulted not from imprudence, but
from unforeseen accidents,—it began running
again as efficiently as before. I continued
my peregrinations to Albany, Buffalo, Detroit,
and Chicago, and other cities in the West
and South.

A VISIT TO THE CAPITAL

AT last we proceeded to the capital of the
United States. Washington is a very attractive city, with superb edifices, wide and well-
paved streets, beautiful shops, and a population of most agreeable quality. It is safe to
say that, after those of Boston, the theater
audiences there are the most intelligent and
appreciative in North America. The delegates to Congress, of the different States,
with their families, form an important contin-

gent of intelligence beyond the average. In
that city I had an experience worth relating.
With an acquaintance who spoke Italian and
English I went one day to visit the Capitol.
When we had entered the majestic structure,
and were walking through the offices, the corridors, and the private rooms of the commit-
tees I noticed that I was an object of curiosity to the many people whom I met. After
half an hour spent in visiting the labyrinth
of halls and galleries, a gentleman presented
himself to me as a member of the House, and
invited me in the name of the Speaker to
visit the House of Representatives. I tried
to excuse myself on the ground of my modest
morning-dress, but the gentleman who invited me observed that this question of dress
was little attended to in America, and I
yielded to his arguments and to those of the
friend who was with me, and presented myself before the Speaker. The Speaker rose
from his chair, as did all the members present. After a few very courteous words, he
gave me permission to visit the hall of the
House, and as I passed through the corridors
between the lines of seats, all the members
advanced from right and left to shake hands

SALVINI AS "OROSMANE" IN THE "ZAÏRE" OF VOLTAIRE.

with me. When I reached the back of the great hall a crowd of the pages of the House, dressed in uniform, surrounded me with little note-books in their hands, belonging to the congressmen, and asked for my autograph. I had to write my name two hundred and seventy-eight times; and, luckily for me, the attendance that day was not large! My hand became cramped with so many signatures, and Heaven knows what my calligraphy became before I finished!

IMPRESSIONS OF EDWIN BOOTH

THE celebrated actor Edwin Booth was at this time in Baltimore, a city distant two hours from the capital. I had heard so much about this superior artist that I was anxious to see him, and on one of my off nights I went to Baltimore with my impresario's agent. A box had been reserved for me without my knowledge, and was draped with the Italian colors. I regretted to be made so conspicuous, but I could not fail to appreciate the courteous and complimentary desire to do me honor shown by the American artist.

It was only natural that I should be most
kindly influenced toward him, but without
the courtesy which predisposed me in his
favor he would equally have won my sympathy by his attractive and artistic linea-
ments, and his graceful and well-proportioned
figure. The play was "Hamlet." This part
brought him great fame, and justly; for in
addition to the high artistic worth with which
he adorned it, his elegant personality was
admirably adapted to it. His long and wavy
hair, his large and expressive eye, his youthful and flexible movements, accorded perfectly with the ideal of the young prince of
Denmark which now obtains everywhere.
His splendid delivery, and the penetrating
philosophy with which he informed his
phrases, were his most remarkable qualities.
I was so fortunate as to see him also as
Richelieu and *Iago*, and in all three of these
parts, so diverse in their character, I found
him absolutely admirable. I cannot say so
much of his *Macbeth*, which I saw one night
when passing through Philadelphia. The
part seemed to me not adapted to his nature.
Macbeth was an ambitious man, and Booth
was not. *Macbeth* had barbarous and fero-

cious instincts, and Booth was agreeable, urbane, and courteous. *Macbeth* destroyed his enemies traitorously,—did this even to gain possession of their goods,—while Booth was noble, lofty-minded, and generous of his wealth. It is thus plain that however much art he might expend, his nature rebelled against his portrayal of that personage, and he could never hope to transform himself into the ambitious, venal, and sanguinary Scottish king.

I should say, from what I heard in America, that Edwin Forrest was the Modena of America. The memory of that actor still lives, for no one has possessed equally the power to give expression to the passions, and to fruitful and burning imagery, in addition to which he possessed astonishing power of voice. Almost contemporaneously a number of most estimable actors have laid claim to his mantle; but above them all Edwin Booth soared as an eagle.

After a very satisfactory experience in Baltimore, I returned for the third time to New York and gave "Othello," "Macbeth," and the "Gladiator," each play twice, and made the last two appearances of my season in Philadelphia. After playing ninety-five times in the new fashion, I felt myself worn out, but fully satisfied with the result of my venturesome undertaking. When I embarked on the steamer which was to take me to Europe, I was escorted by all the artists of the company which had coöperated in my happy success, by my friends, and by courteous admirers, and I felt that if I were not an Italian I should wish to be an American.

IN EGYPT

AT the end of May, 1881, I landed at Havre, and went on to Paris, where I took a good week of rest—relative rest, that is, for in that city it is not easy to do nothing. I did not fail to frequent the Comédie Française to hear some of those excellent society comedies which are played there with so much taste, delicacy, and truth; and after having myself recited such a vast quantity of verse during seven months, that pure and beautiful prose appeared to me a most savory change, seasoned as it was with the most delicate sauces and spices by the most expert of

cooks. When I reached Florence my first
thought was to retire at once to my country
house, to enjoy that calm which one cannot
find except at home and in the bosom of his
family. However, offers of new theatrical enterprises came to disturb my repose, and I
was constrained to accept a proposition that
I should go to Egypt for the months of
December, 1881, and January, 1882. I
formed, for these two months only, an Italian
company, and on December 3 I opened in
Alexandria. Theatrical methods there are
regulated upon the Italian principles, and it
is necessary to change the play every night;
so besides my accustomed tragedies I gave
dramas and comedies, as, for example, "Le
Lapidaire," by Alexandre Dumas; "Fasma,"
by Dall' Ongaro; "La Calomnie," by Scribe;
and "La Suonatrice d'Arpa," by Chiossone.

I need not say how much pleasure the
people of Alexandria took in these plays.
The Italian colony overwhelmed me with
generous demonstrations, and the Boat Club
invited me to name after myself a new acquisition of their navy — not, it is true, a
Duilio. After playing fourteen times in
Alexandria, we went to Cairo, and I lost no

14*

time in visiting those tremendous monuments
the Pyramids, glorious and imposing relics of
a greatness the idea of which we cannot now
even conceive.

RECEPTION IN RUSSIA

At the end of January I went back to
Italy, and was invited to go to Russia. I got
together fresh actors and actresses, and on
February 24, 1882, I presented myself on the
stage of the Maria Theater in St. Petersburg.
I thus passed quickly from a land of suffocating heat to one of bitter cold, but changes of
temperature have never affected me much.
I confess that when I first entered that em-
pire I had a vague apprehension, the cause
of which I did not fully explain to myself.
I had been invited by the Direction of the
Imperial Theaters, I came in the quality of
a foreign artist, and no harm could possi-
bly come to me; nevertheless, after the vex-
ations inflicted by the customs officers at the
Russian frontier on the members of my company, an indescribable disgust developed in
my mind. My imagination is naturally fer-

vid, and in my fancy I saw the poor exiles in
Siberia, the knout administered in the public
streets to disrespectful subjects, the tortures
of the prisons, the summary confiscations of
the property of the suspected, the arrogance
of the soldiery, the extreme rigor of the laws,
the servile obsequiousness obligatory toward
the Czar, the despotism of the great, and the
extreme degradation of the humble; and all
this seemed to me so dark as in fact to be
wholly black. The Nihilists had only a little
before laid their inexorable hand on their
prey, and all were still palpitating with the
tragic end of the Emperor Alexander II.
You can imagine how the Government stood
to its arms, and how the people constantly
trembled with dread. The theater was a permitted and innocent distraction, and there,
freed from fear, and laying aside the pertur-
bation of politics, the public worked off its excitement in clamorous enthusiasm, sometimes
to the point of disturbing the course of the
play and disconcerting the unlucky actor. I
have never had experience with a public so
systematically persistent in applause as the
Russian. After the artist has gone through
a very fatiguing part, and, panting, pros-

trated, in a bath of perspiration, hopes to
be able to retire to his room to rest, he is
obliged to stand for a full half-hour, exhausted
and perspiring as he is, to receive the inter-
minable ovations of the people; and he must
go before the curtain fifteen, twenty, or even
thirty times.   Not content with that, they
wait for you at the door, no matter how long
you take to dress, and stand in lines for you
to pass between, begging a look or a touch
of your hand; and if you live so near by as
not to need a carriage, they accompany you
on foot to the door of your lodgings, with
open manifestations of sympathy.   The Russian is courteous, hospitable, liberal to the
actor; but, like all those whose enthusiasm
exceeds due bounds, he forgets easily.

There have been but very few native artists
of celebrity.   On the other hand, the Imperial
companies, which play only in St. Petersburg
and Moscow, are meritorious, and distinguished for the smoothness of their representations.   In the secondary cities the artistic
contingent is of wretched quality, and may
be compared with the lowest ranks of our
own—the so-called *guitti;* but the Russian public, particularly in the provinces, is

amiable, tolerant, and ready, for the sake of amusement of any kind, to accept an alloy for the pure metal. I made twenty appearances at St. Petersburg in thirty-eight days, and then went to Moscow, where I gave eleven more performances. At Moscow the public seemed to be much calmer, and, moreover, our houses were much better. In both cities splendid gifts were made me, which I preserve as pleasant remembrances of an enjoyable experience. By the end of April, 1882, I was again resting in Florence.

STUDY OF "KING LEAR"

AFTER having given due attention to the interests of my family, and fulfilled my social obligations, I employed my time in polishing my study of Shakspere's *King Lear*, and overcoming some difficulties which that character presented to me, with the intention of bringing it out in the United States, whither I had arranged to go in the beginning of October. My work on that day preoccupied me greatly, and although I had brought it out in a preliminary appearance at the Teatro Salvini, and it had been well received by public and press, I did not feel entirely satisfied with myself, and I proposed to combat my difficulties deliberately and seriously. I wished to find the way to make some scenes more effective, while maintaining the character in its proper relations. It was necessary to devise means for producing effects with auxiliaries different from those to which I had been accustomed, to move and interest the audience by creating new combinations and contrasts, and by conjuring up a type of sentiment in accord with the character and the age of that grandiose personage. I do not know whether I was successful, but the greeting of the public gave me assurance that I made at least some approach to my object. I was thus provided with a new play for my third venture in the United States.

I played 109 times in this season as against 95 the time before; moreover, the last sixteen representations of the " Morte Civile" were most lucrative, since I gave them in company with the famous actress Clara Morris. It is right that I should pay a merited tribute to this excellent actress; for one could not wish for a better interpreter of the part of *Rosalia* in the drama I have named. This season was also more brilliant than the one before it, because the rumor had spread that I would not come again to North America—a baseless and absurd rumor, since the financial results were rather such as to encourage me to cross the ocean again, as in fact they did. The public was, however, so fully persuaded of the sincerity of my alleged resolution, that several gentlemen associated themselves to offer me a banquet at the Hotel Brunswick, at which all classes of New York society were represented. The distinguished German actor Barnay, who was then in New York, came to the banquet after his play, and made a speech full of kindly encomium, which aroused sincere enthusiasm.

I again recrossed the ocean, not to rest, as I might perhaps have been excused for doing, after so many and continuous fatigues, but to study the part of *Coriolanus* in proof of my unwearied love of my art, which I have always looked upon as my second mother. If in the vicissitudes of my life I had not had this recourse, I do not know what would have become of me. Art has always received me, restored me, protected me; and if it has not been able to make me forget my misfortunes altogether, it has mitigated them. I owe to it my moments of comfort, satisfaction, and joy, and now that I am constrained to abandon it, I do not weep, for I have never been weak; but my heart feels the sting of bitterness.

While I was occupying myself with the character of that impetuous but valorous warrior, it was proposed to me to go to Rome and Trieste, and to play a few times in Florence. My fellow-citizens never evinced more affection and admiration for me than upon this occasion. At Rome my nine appearances were greeted with hearty interest and enthusiasm. At Florence the theater was never large enough to receive those who wished to secure entrance, and at Trieste I was overwhelmed with ovations. The same company went with me for a season at Covent Garden, London. The time of the year was not propitious. At the end of February there were very thick fogs accompanying a humid and cold atmosphere, and the heating arrangements of the theater were so defective that it seemed like playing in an ice-house. I remember that on the night when I played the " Gladiator," in the fourth act, when I had to fight in the arena with nothing but silken tights on my body, before I went on my teeth chattered with cold. At the end of that very fatiguing act the perspiration rolled from me as in a Turkish bath, and when I reached my dressing-room a heavy chill came over me, from the effects of which I suffered long. The audience sat in their overcoats and furs, the men with their collars turned up, and the women with their heads wrapped in shawls and hoods. Our season had opened with excellent promise, but whatever may have been the public's love for the theater, many were constrained to stay away in such weather for fear of illness. I made urgent complaints to my impresario, but the evil was irremediable. After twenty-one nights of " Othello," " King Lear," " Macbeth," the " Gladiator," and " Hamlet," we proceeded to Edinburgh, and the weather having become milder, our business again rose to its regular level. Our tour included the cities of Glasgow, Manchester, Newcastle, Birmingham, Brighton, and Dublin, and closed with a farewell representation of " Othello " in London.

"CORIOLANUS"

IT being out of the question to remain in
London, the only city in which a summer
season is possible, I proposed to my company
that they should continue at my disposition
at half salary from the end of May until
November 1 of that year (1884), proposing
again to go on the road at the latter date.
They agreed; and on November 4 we began
a series of nine representations at Naples,
whence we went to Messina, Palermo, and
Catania, and thus I ended the year, resolved
to confine myself for the immediate future to
the study of the banished and vindictive hero
Coriolanus. I felt that I could divine that
character, which resembled my own in some
ways—not, certainly, in his warlike exploits,
but in his susceptibility, in his spurning of
the arrogance and insolent pretensions of the
ignorant masses, and, above all, in his filial
submissiveness and affection.   Unfortunately,
I was not able to submit the results of this
study to the judgment of the Italian public,
as I have done with all my others, since it
demands too costly a stage setting, and it was

impossible to secure in the great number of assistants that artistic discipline without which the grandiose easily merges in the ridiculous. I regretted this much, as my compatriots would have given me an unbiased and intellectual judgment of the work; but for the reasons I have stated I reconciled myself to giving it for the first time at the Metropolitan Opera House in New York, where, indeed, nothing was lacking for an admirable setting of the tragedy. This, as my reader will not need to be told, was the fourth time that I went before the American public, on three of which times I was supported by an English-speaking company.

The close of my artistic career approaches, and with it the end of the anecdotes with which it has been diversified. The chief object of these memoirs is to make it known to any one whom it may aid how a young man, without inherited resources, and constrained to look out for himself from very early years, can, by upright conduct, firm resolution, and assiduous effort, acquire in time some renown, and the means for enjoying the comforts of life in his old age without being dependent on anybody. Those who meet with misfortune owing to too little application to study, or to pretensions out of proportion to their deserts, deserve indulgence indeed, but not compassion. If my example can be of utility to those who are born with artistic instincts, I shall have the reward for which I hoped in undertaking this sketch of my life. Moralizing is now out of fashion, but an example still receives attention, and may be of service. Art is pure, loyal, honorable, uncontaminated. Through these virtues it exacts, commands, imposes morality upon whomsoever places himself under its ægis, and it rejects, condemns, and punishes him who fails to respect it. It is for this reason that great artists, with rare exceptions, are moral and honorable.

A LUDICROUS APPEARANCE IN KHARKOV

BEFORE telling of my fourth visit to North America, I must narrate a rather strange experience which I had in the spring of 1885. A lady (I say *lady* to distinguish the sex) made me an offer to play in Little Russia with native actors. My knowledge of all foreign languages is extremely limited, but of Russian I do not know a single word. I informed my would-be impresario of this difficulty, and she diminished my hesitation by writing me that Italian was more or less familiar to all in those regions, and particularly at Kharkov, where there is a university, and that the actors would do their best to coöperate with me; and she added that she would provide two prompters speaking the two languages. Persistence sometimes overcomes even avarice, and I allowed myself to be seduced by her pressing arguments. I went to Kharkov, where the company was assembled, and I was scandalized to behold a theater entirely of wood, old, ruinous, and littered with the dirt of a century, which was enough to make me shiver. The actors, except the leading lady, who could recognize French by sight, did not understand a word outside of their own tongue; there were indeed two prompters, but the Russian knew no Italian, and the Italian no Russian. At the rehearsals the two prompters made a conventional sign to each other to call the attention of the one upon whom it was incumbent to speak. The actors, who were Russian pro-

15

vincials, seemed not to be in the habit of
committing their parts to memory, for even
at the last rehearsal which I made with them,
they were not sure of their lines. The unhappy prompter had to repeat a phrase two
and three times to get the actor to take it,
and you can imagine what smoothness this
system produced in the representation. I am
naturally patient, and I sought to inculcate
into this band of mountebanks the advantages
of more study, more exactness, more attention, and I sought to furnish them with an
example by never giving the Italian prompter
occasion to speak; but it profited nothing.
The public representation began, and the
audience, accustomed to that system of acting,
was not at all disturbed by it, but seemed to
look upon it as a surprising phenomenon that,
while the murmur of the prompter formed a
constant accompaniment to the words of the
other actors, when I spoke the murmur ceased.
It seemed, too, that little attention was given
to exactness in costume, for I noticed that
Brabantio in "Othello" wore short breeches
and shoes with buckles, like a priest. In
the "Gladiator," instead of tunic and toga,
the lover came on the stage in trunk-hose

and short Spanish cloak of the time of Philip II. You can picture to yourself what the scenery, furniture, and accessories must have been. But the people did not complain, and did not even criticize. In their eyes everything was admirable, and they gave vent to the most exaggerated enthusiasm. During the rehearsals the prompters occupied stools, one on each side of the stage, but during the public performances both crowded into the little prompter's box, which was covered with a hood of pasteboard. On the first night I was so much preoccupied that I thought of nothing that did not concern the course of the play itself, but on the second I noticed those two unfortunates wedged in together, simply melting with perspiration, each with one arm out of the box holding the book of the play, and nudging each other at intervals to indicate whose turn it was to prompt; and, thinking of the Siamese twins, such an impulse to laugh came upon me that with difficulty I avoided making a scandal.

The University of Kharkov is large and of much importance, and, as was natural, the audiences were made up in large part of students. Every one knows the characteristics of that picked class of society, marked by energy, enthusiasm, goodness of heart, and generous tendencies, compounded with thoughtlessness and disorder. Especially in Russia, where the students are held in check by a rigorous Government, which suppresses every liberal aspiration, whenever an opportunity offers to give rein to excitement, the reaction follows, and unbridled demonstrations break out. I refer to this because one night I had experience of the consequences of this condition. I do not remember what the play was, but when I came out of the theater I found a real mob waiting for me, and with deafening shouts they lifted me in the air and carried me above their heads like a balloon to my carriage, into which they threw me as if I were a rubber ball. I may remark that I weigh 250 pounds! As soon as I felt myself freed from their clutches, I shouted, "Whip up, driver!" and the horses broke into a trot; but the crowd ran behind the carriage shouting and clamoring, and from time to time I caught the words "*Un souvenir!*" It was not easy for me to satisfy them at that moment, but a happy idea came to me. When I reached my hotel I remembered that I had in my portfolio a number of visiting-cards. I took them all and threw them into the most fervent group of manifesters, and while these were busy picking up the cards, I had time to get out of my carriage and rush into the hotel, happy in my deliverance. The Russians are most lavish in their gifts, and I brought away many as remembrances of those regions, which I have not seen since. At Saratov and at Taganrog there was no lack of demonstrations; but as there were no students, enthusiasm did not become dangerous to life, as in Kharkov. We were to have gone on to Kazan, but the manager thought it good to pocket all the receipts, and to omit to pay the actors, who justly refused to keep on under these conditions. I gave a performance for their benefit, and took my departure, leaving that management of little faith the richer by several thousands of francs on my account also, but very glad, nevertheless, to get away from it.

MISFORTUNES IN CALIFORNIA

From my journey to Russia I returned to Florence, to await the time of going to the United States, where the season opened,

15'

as usual, in the month of October. My first performances were in the new Metropolitan Opera House. There I first produced "Cori- olanus," and I was so happy as to meet with a flattering reception. After the usual tour through the chief cities, in February, 1886, we went to California. The weather was un- usually severe. Along the line beyond Den- ver was erected an immense penthouse of wood, many miles long, to carry over the tracks the frequent avalanches from the mountains above. To admire this Titanic work I went out on the platform of my car before we reached the entrance of the snow- shed, and for more than half an hour I was compelled to breathe the damp cloud of smoke and steam, which was shut in by the shed and could not escape. I say I was *forced* to breathe it, because in the darkness and the dazed feeling produced by the dense and black atmosphere, and the undulation of the swiftly running train, I was afraid to move for fear of falling on the rails. When we shot out into the light I was as drenched as if I had been ducked in a well, and I believe it is to this that I owe the complete loss of my voice after our first two or three performances in San Francisco,—a thing which in my whole career had never happened to me before. It was a most provoking accident. Everything promised us at the outset a splendid financial success,—my artistic success was won already,—when the sudden closing of the theater, the uncertainty of the people whether I could go on again, and the contemporaneous appearance of several new attractions, all united to divert the public from us, and we passed a week of interrupted profit and unlooked-for loss. I tried the most heroic and disagreeable remedies, but the disease would not be turned from its course, and we had to wait until my vocal organs could resume their sonority. While I lay in bed trying to get well, out of spirits, cross, and worried, not only for my own loss, but for that of my manager, a telegraphic despatch came from Florence to aggravate my trouble and grieve me sorely. My brother Alessandro was dead. This sad news pained and depressed me so greatly that when I returned to the stage, not fully cured, and afflicted by my sudden loss, the public could not have formed a very favorable opinion of my artistic merit. Certainly I was not in condition to make the most of what I may have had.

PLAYING WITH BOOTH

FROM California we returned to New York, where I had an offer to play for three weeks with the famous artist Edwin Booth, to give three performances of "Othello" a week, with Booth as *Iago* and me as *Othello*. The cities selected were New York, Philadelphia, and Boston. As the managers had to hire the theaters by the week, they proposed that we should give "Hamlet" as a fourth performance, with Booth as *Hamlet* and me as the *Ghost*. I accepted with the greatest pleasure, flattered to be associated with so distinguished and sympathetic an artist. I cannot find epithets to characterize those twelve performances! The word "extraordinary" is not enough, nor is "splendid"; I will call them "unique," for I do not believe that any similar combination has ever aroused such interest in North America. To give some idea of it, I will say that the receipts for the twelve performances were $43,500, an average of $3,625 a night. In

Italy such receipts would be something phe-
nomenal; in America they were very satisfactory. During this time I came to know
Booth, and I found in him every quality that
can characterize a gentleman. The affability
and modesty of his manners rendered him
justly loved and esteemed, not only by his
countrymen, but by all who had the fortune
to make his acquaintance. For the performances I have described, the best-known artists
who were then free were engaged; and my
son Alessandro played *Cassio* in "Othello"
and *Laertes* in "Hamlet" with honor to himself, as he had also played with credit in more
important parts in the course of my tour.
This still youthful actor was endowed by nature with the gift of easily acquiring north-
ern idioms. He was educated in German
Switzerland, and had made a thorough study
of German, which rendered the acquisition
of English easy for him. I had sought to
influence him in any other direction than
that of the stage, but in a few months he ventured to present himself before the New
York public in a lover's part, in English, beside that able actress Clara Morris, and the
verdict was encouraging. By degrees he

mastered the English language to such a degree that it could not be perceived that he was a foreigner.   Nature bestowed upon this youth the material of an actor.   He has a good presence, a fine voice, a vivid imagination, and a natural adaptability to diverse characters.   In my opinion those best suited to him are the virile and energetic; in the languid, amorous, and sentimental he does not seem to me so successful.

FIFTH VISIT TO THE UNITED STATES

In 1889 I accepted a fifth engagement for North America.   The actor's life in North America can be summed up in three words, "Theater, railroad, hotel."   Very few are the cities in which a stop of two or three weeks is made.   Away from the large centers, sometimes theater and town are changed every night, with the intervening weariness of packing and of sleeping-cars.   And in addition there is the infliction of the reporters, to which you must submit, the thousands of autographs from which there is no relief, and the admirers who persecute you.   As you can imagine, at the end of such a season of seven months the actor is very eager to tear this shirt of Nessus from his back. But with all that, if I had been ten years younger I should have returned thither ten times more. One can endure in America what would not be endurable in Europe, and especially in Italy. I do not know whether this is due to the air, or to the material comforts of life, or whether it is that the example of industry animates, fortifies, and spurs one on : but it is certain that so continuous a strain in Europe would prostrate a man in a single year, while in America, one undergoes it with resignation and resists it with courage. I will not deny that the anticipation of a satisfactory profit had some influence in maintaining my vitality, although my strongest incitement came from knowing that I was appreciated and loved.

"SAMSON"

IN October, 1889, then, I found myself again in North America, and I began again the life which I have described. This time, too, I was fortunate in the choice of a play

which I had already given in the United
States during my first visit in 1873 with
the Italian company. After seventeen years
"Samson" could be called new to the audiences who saw it. This play was put on
the stage as a great spectacle. Scenery,
furniture, costumes, accessories, all were
made new for the occasion. The fall of the
temple of Dagon was presented with so
much realism that I feared every night that
I should be crushed under one of those
enormous blocks which fell on all sides of
me. My son Alessandro had the stage management, and he took diligent precautions
against a catastrophe. Nevertheless, one
night a block of cornice rebounded, and gave
me a bruise on the leg which lasted for
several days. I was fortunate in having in
the actress who played *Delilah* a most effi-
cient coadjutress in the great success of that
tragedy. During seven consecutive months
I gave only three plays—"Othello," "Samson," and the "Gladiator," except that in the
last month I added the "Morte Civile," to be
able to take a little breath, and played it
as a rest. I gave "Othello" thirty-six times,
"Samson" thirty-five, the "Gladiator"

twenty, and the "Morte Civile" twelve,—in all one hundred and three performances, all requiring great expenditure of force. I need hardly say that, as always, the public showed me appreciation beyond my deserts.

I realized, however, that I should not have the courage to make a sixth appearance in America under those inexorable conditions, and I resolved to announce my farewell to the American people in the papers, with expression of my regret at taking my leave of them for the last time. No one would believe my declaration. People adduced the example of other artists, who have used this means to swell their audiences; but to the honor of truth I can say that I never was under the necessity of having recourse to so puerile a subterfuge. I was induced to say adieu to the United States by my fear of being no longer able to answer their expectation, for it had cost me too much to hide the extreme fatigue consequent on my performances during the season just expired. In former years, owing to my exuberant strength, every effort came spontaneously; now I felt that, to attain the same effects, I must make a greater expenditure of energy. As I left that hospitaable land behind, and saw the great Statue of Liberty fade gradually from my sight, I felt a pang in my soul, and if my eyes were dry, my heart wept. I made a salute to that country whose people are so full of vigor, industry, and courage, and lack neither culture, nor understanding, nor feeling. May the United States receive the salutation of a humble artist, who while his heart beats will feel for that nation respect and love!

In returning to Europe the thought consoled me that I left in the land of Washington an offshoot of my blood. My son Alessandro loves the United States as I do, and can henceforth call himself half American; and I am sure that with industry and unflinching will, besides winning general estimation for himself, he will keep alive beyond the ocean a sympathetic memory of me. In the mean time, thank God, he represents me worthily, and through him my name is still heard in America.

IAGO

In 1890–91 Andrea Maggi's company was at the Teatro Niccolini in Florence for the carnival season. Maggi had played the part of *Othello* in other cities, and every condition seemed to favor my taking that of *Iago* in that theater, one of those of the highest repute in Italy. I accepted, and set to work to study, not the character, which was already impressed on my mind, but the mechanism of the words, a thing which for some little time had become difficult for me, owing to a defect of memory. It was much harder for me to commit exactly to memory the precise lines of the part of *Iago* than to form a conception of the personage and to study out the effects. As to the last, the best way to arrive at many is to seek for none. This is not the place to make an analysis of the character; I will only say that every one looks at it in his own way, and that I have already published my view of it. The "actor of the classic school," as some impressionists call me, aimed to present an example of naturalness in delivery, while bringing into relief the poetic beauties of the part, and to effect this so that the verse form should not obscure truth; and it is said that success was not lacking. With this interpretation I completed my trilogy of parts of the second rank, the others being *Lanciotto* in "Francesca da Rimini" and *Pylades* in "Oreste"; and it was my purpose with these to demonstrate that even in an inferior part it is entirely possible to win the consideration of the public.

It has always been my aim to overcome the difficulties of my profession. The more difficult a thing has seemed, the more firmly I have set my mind upon conquering it. Not a few of the characters which I have played in the course of my long career have aroused bitter criticism, and yet have been well received by the public because my interpretation has been found accurate. Others have dated their success from some counsel of mine, which was based on experience, and for which the author has been grateful to me. Has the collection of the masterworks of art always found in me an interpreter of mirror-like truth? No, I say. I have sought to the extent that my limited abilities have permitted to penetrate to my author's ideal, but I have the conscience to confess that I have not always risen to the height of my own conception. I have never had a more severe critic than myself in matters pertaining to my art. As I myself look at it, my sentiment of blame is stronger than that of satisfaction.